Stepping Off the Porch

By Amy Watkins

Copyrights and Permissions

This novel is a work of fiction. Yes, I was born and raised in Washington, DC, but mom, I promise I never snuck out the house to go to a club. Any other resemblance to situations or persons living or dead are also coincidence and are the work of the author's very vivid imagination.

Dedication

To God for his mercy and grace. For forgiving me every time I fell short. For comforting me when I was heartbroken. For retrieving me when I was lost in the deepest darkest labyrinth. For providing me with talents and provoking me to share. For His love, peace, and inspiration. Thank You!

"So flee youthful passions and pursue righteousness, faith, love, and peace, along with those who call on the Lord from a pure heart. Have nothing to do with foolish, ignorant controversies; you know that they breed quarrels. And the Lord's servant must not be quarrelsome but kind to everyone, able to teach, patiently enduring evil, correcting his opponents with gentleness. God may perhaps grant them repentance leading to a knowledge of the truth, and they may come to their senses and escape from the snare of the devil, after being captured by him to do his will."

2Timothy 2:22-26

Chapter 1 – Lovey in September 1998

I was born and raised in Washington, DC when it was live. A few decades prior, riots conquered U Street and gave DC the much-deserved nickname, Chocolate City. A few decades after, gentrification won the city back. But in 1998, DC was at its prime. I was sixteen and it was midnight. I walked down a city block with my best friend Erica by my side. Trey, our seventeen-year-old neighbor, had just dropped us off on the corner of 9th and E Street and then went in search of a parking spot. The booming bass from a car radio filled the air - the mating call of the hood.

"Ay, shorty," a deep inviting voice from the black BMW rang out.

"Haaaaay," Erica and I called back in unison.

We were young, wild, and free - escaping from the domains of our safe abodes we called home. Our adult bodies were our tickets to fun. We skipped the long line outside of the nightclub and got in without monetary charge, our entrance fee covered by our revealing outfits.

The club was blasting with go-go, music indigenous to DC. Band members were center stage banging on drums and rapping into a microphone, all swaying side to side in unison. Go-go music started off loud, fast-paced and raw, and it maintained that energy all night long. The dance of us natives matched the music's energy. Shaking, grinding, and winding formed the basis of these animated dance moves. The club was so hot and humid from the excessive workout that the walls were sweating and the ceiling rained from condensation. A black mosh pit formed in the center of the room. Energized Black men, chiseled and shirtless, jumped around and bumped into each other. They represented their cliques with hand signals and shout-outs.

Erica and I engaged in the festivities from the center of the chaos. I was a virgin, but nevertheless, I knew how to sway my hips to the beat of the drum. A man twice my age held my waist and swayed his hips to compliment my grind.

Erica, at fifteen, already had many men under her belt and was being hoisted up by a handsome young creature who had her legs wrapped around his waist like a belt. Thankfully, I convinced her to wear shorts that night instead of the short miniskirt she had considered.

"Ay, what you doing with my cousin?" Trey said, trying to intimidate handsome.

We hadn't even noticed that he'd come into the club until he spoke from right beside us. Trey had always been protective of Erica and I. Erica was not related to him, but you wouldn't know that by looking at them. They both had smooth chocolate skin, brown eyes, and deep dimples. They differed in stature, however. Erica was five foot two, thin, and had large breasts. Trey was six foot two and thick.

"Chill Trey," Erica responded before handsome could.

A smile crept across Trey's face as he locked eyes with Erica. Erica gazed back, a warning sign in her eyes that said not to do what she knew he would.

"She's fifteen," Trey announced, and Erica's scowl intensified.

"My bad shorty," handsome said as he lowered Erica to her feet. "You fine and all, but I am not trying to catch a case."

Handsome ran away faster than a roach when the lights come on.

Erica was naturally hot headed and spunky. I knew she was about to tell Trey off in front of the entire club so I decided to intervene before she made a scene. I released the grip of whoever was holding me and positioned myself between Erica and Trey.

"Dance with me Trey," I said as I wrapped my arms around his neck and started winding.

I could feel Erica behind me speaking to Trey with her eyes, *"You are so lucky."* Trey smiled deeper as he wrapped his arms around my waist and moved with me.

Trey had a crush on me since the third grade and Erica always tried to play matchmaker, but previously, I wasn't interested. He started out a weakly looking kid, short and skinny, with jagged teeth and thick glasses. But he had grown into a fine muscular hunk of a man. In middle school he got braces which straightened his teeth nicely. And he tossed his glasses for contacts that added an extra sparkle to his beautiful eyes. When he flashed a smile at me, my heart melted. And up until that point, I never let him know it.

"I want you," I whispered into his ear.

His chest was pressed so close to mine that I could feel his heartbeat skip. His waist was so close to mine that I could feel his manhood grow. For a second, it was just us on the dance floor. We slow danced and swayed in the middle of madness.

He didn't say anything. He just smiled and inched his hands down to my buttocks. When I didn't push him away, he bent down and kissed me. And there we were open-mouthed and tongue in the middle of the dance floor at a DC nightclub. I had never felt a kiss so warm, soft, and inviting. A spark grew out of the pit of my stomach and trickled down between my legs.

If my parents knew what I was doing they would have grabbed me by the ear, whipped my butt in the middle of the club and grounded me until I graduated college. They were so strict. I wasn't allowed to play video games, watch mature movies, or go out to parties. The only social events they even considered me partaking in were school related functions. And a boyfriend, that would have been absolutely out of the question.

"At sixteen, you don't need to focus on boys right now," they often reminded me if I even looked in the direction of a young man. "All you need to focus on is your schoolwork." They wanted me to stay a virgin forever. But I was ready. I hated living under their roof with their rules and their ways.

I had Erica though - my way out. We had been best friends since kindergarten. Our backyards shared the same alley. That's how we met. I was playing outside in the back yard when this wild haired, wide-eyed girl hopped over the fence and introduced herself. From then on, we were inseparable. Either I was spending the night over at her house or she was spending the night at mine. And often during those sleep overs we'd sneak out and hang out with the fellas around our neighborhood or make our way to a club.

"Tear the club up! Tear the club up!" the lead singer raged through the microphone.

The crowd's energy went from 80 to 100. People jumped and stomped around as if they were trying to take all the stress that had accumulated over the week out on the floor. Trey and I broke our intimate hold to join in with the ruckus.

A fight broke out between two guys yards away from us. Trey, Erica, and I witnessed blows to the face and abdomen as a circle formed around the two. Security elbowed their way through the crowd to grab the troublemakers and escort them out of the building.

"Ay," the lead singer of the band shouted into his microphone, "if ya'll keep that shit up we not gonna play. Are we good?"

"Yeah," the crowd responded.

"Are we good!?"

"Yeah!" the crowd shouted louder.

"Well alright then," and he signaled his band members to start again. "Tear the club up! Tear the club up!"

And everyone was back dancing and shouting like nothing had ever happened.

We partied until the lights in the club came on and the announcement, "You ain't got to go home but you gotta get the hell out of here!" was made. Most people would head to IHOP or Ben's Chili Bowl for a snack, but we had to go home. Erica's mom would soon be up trying to get us ready for church. I grabbed Trey's left hand and Erica's right and we made our way through the crowd to the exit.

Thank God the parking spot Trey found was only a couple of blocks away. My feet were killing me in my three-inch heels. As soon as we hopped in the car I took those bad boys off my feet and gave myself a massage.

"You've got some pretty feet Lovey," Trey said to me.

"Thanks boo," I blushed.

Erica rolled her eyes.

It didn't take us long to get back uptown to our neighborhood. Trey turned down Notorious BIG's Big Papa which was booming on the radio when we pulled up to our block. He parked his car at the entrance way to alley between Erica's house and mine.

"Mom's light isn't on. I think we made it," Erica mentioned, but her words fell on deaf ears because Trey and I were already fully engaged in a seductive goodnight kiss. Erica sucked her teeth and rolled her eyes at us. "Get a room!"

Trey didn't expect me to abruptly break away from the kiss so he continued to kiss the air for a split second after I broke which made me giggle.

"Huh, come on Lovey. We gotta get in the house before mom wakes up."

"Alright! Alright!" I responded.

"You gonna call me tomorrow?" Trey asked.

"You know it." I gave him a peck and got out of the car to meet Erica who was already standing and impatiently tapping her foot. Trey watched as we made our way down the dark alley. When we got out of earshot of Trey Erica wrapped her arm around my shoulder.

"You know I slept with him, right?" she whispered.

"Slept with who?"

"With Trey."

My vision started to tunnel after I heard her words. I was stunned and hurt. I brushed the feeling of doom off and tried to pretend like I was not phased.

"What? You never told me that."

"Yeah, I did. Last summer, remember? The guy that couldn't figure out which way the condom went because he was so nervous."

"That was Trey?" I remembered her telling me about this encounter but I didn't know it was Trey. I was disgusted at myself for even thinking about losing my virginity to someone my girl had already fucked. That would have been a disastrous break in the girl code.

"Yeah, that was Trey. But it was nothing. I don't care if you date him. Besides, you need someone to give your little cookie too. You holdin' onto that virginity of yours like it's some special prize."

When I was younger, I fantasized a lot about my first time. I wanted it to be special. I would lose my virginity to Mr. Perfect. He'd have perfect skin, perfect teeth, be the perfect height, have the perfect muscular build, and he'd always know the right things to say. He'd be romantic and sweet to me, but strong and bold enough to protect me from everybody else. And he'd love me unconditionally. I planned the entire night in my head. Mr. Perfect and I would have a fun-filled romantic date at the most expensive restaurant in town where we'd talk and laugh for hours. Then he'd take me to a five-star hotel where rose petals and chocolate treats covered the bed. He'd make love to me and then promise to take care of me and love me forever.

But, at 16, I was tired of waiting for Mr. Perfect. I wanted to experience full on womanhood. I hoped that Trey would take me on that ride. I pondered Erica giving me permission to hook up with Trey, but I decided against it.

"Naw, that's alright. I don't want your sloppy seconds," I teased and we both laughed.

By that time, we'd made it to Erica's basement door. The door creaked open and we held our breath as we walked inside. King, Erica's German shepherd let out a few deep barks.

"Shhh King, it's me," Erica said trying to keep him quiet. But it was too late. We heard footsteps from above and saw the light turn on at the top of the basement steps.

"Erica!" called Ms. Decker from above. "What are you guys doing down there that got King all hyped up."

"Shit!" I whispered as Erica and I were still fully adorned in club attire and make-up. All Ms. Decker had to do was walk a few feet and we'd be caught. I would be grounded for the rest of my life. I was shaking. But Erica remained calm, as usual.

"Nothing ma!" Erica responded. "You know that dog has nightmares sometimes and barks in his sleep. Go back to bed. You know we got church in the morning."

We heard Ms. Decker mumble some probably choice words then she slammed the basement door shut. I was able to breathe again.

"Damn, you always so jumpy," Erica said. My claws were still digging into her arm. She shook it free. "Come on, let's get out of these clothes."

We changed into our pajamas and went to bed. Erica fell asleep immediately, but I couldn't sleep. I tossed and turned thinking about Trey. I liked him a lot. But I couldn't be with him after Erica had. I grew angry thinking about how promiscuous Erica was and how there would be nothing left for me if I waited for someone she hadn't been with. She had probably screwed everyone in the metropolitan area. I thought about how maybe I should be selfish and fuck Trey anyway. I mean Erica had plenty of guys, she wouldn't miss one, right? And she said she didn't care.

I realized how stupid I was being. There would be someone out there for me. The right one. I just had to be patient. And with that insight I finally drifted off to sleep. But no less than an hour later Ms. Decker was shaking me, trying to wake me up.

"Time for church! Get up!" she stated as she shook us.

I immediately rose, but Erica rolled over.

"Ma, just give us five more minutes please."

"Nope, I already gave you ten. Time to get up now. I am not trying to be late for service. You know how I love hearing the praise team."

It was more like, Ms. Decker loved looking at the praise team. She had a crush on the tenor who always sat in the center third row. None of us knew his name but she called him her chocolate dip. Matter of fact, Ms. Decker wasn't really a church girl at all. We only went because she was hoping to catch a nice good Christian man she could wrap her legs and heart around. She wanted a man desperately and church was her fishing grounds. She made sure she looked top notch each Sunday. Hair, nails and makeup were always freshly done and from the usher at the beginning of service to the tithe collector at the end of service, she was flirting. Most women we interacted with kept their men held close to them. You'd frequently see some guy getting smacked on the back of the head with their wife's purse for looking in Ms. Decker's direction. She was a beautiful woman. Brown skin, deep dimples and the perfect hourglass figure. Every outfit she wore tightly hugged her body and showed off her greatest assets.

I thought church was boring. We'd sit there for hours listening to a pastor preach about stuff that didn't even apply to our lives. Ms. Decker seemed to like it. She was usually very attentive to the pastor's words and would often shout, "Yes" or "Amen" at pivotal points.

Erica hated church. She always gave her mom the biggest attitude when she was forced to go. There was a lot of eye rolling and teeth sucking through the sermon. She'd always sit slouched down in her seat with her arms folded. Ms. Decker tried to convince her to sit straight and listen, but Erica never complied.

"Why do you hate church so much?" I asked Erica after we returned to her house that Sunday.

"Girl, me and my mom done been to so many churches. Every time my mom breaks up with some dude she been dating at our church we head to another church. I been to dozens and ain't none of them good. You got the fire and brimstone preachers, you know the ones that say if you are gay you're going to hell, if you have sex you're going to hell, if you talk back to your mom you're going to hell, if you lie or cheat or steal or eat the wrong food you're going to hell. Well, that don't make sense cause we've all done something bad so that means we're all going to hell and no one is going to heaven?

"Then you got the prosperity preachers, you know the ones that say if you give me all your money and have enough faith whatever you're praying for will happen. You can find the perfect man, you can heal from cancer, and you can get that job, big house, and fancy car that you've been coveting. *'You just have to believe, and you will receive,'*" Erica mocked in her best old preacher voice. "Well, that's bullshit, 'cause my mom's been giving all her money and praying every night for years but she still ain't found a good man to marry.

"Then you got the all sins forgiven preachers. Those the ones that beat up on their wives, sleep around, lie, cheat, and steal all week long then Sunday they come to church claiming that because they believe in Jesus they are forgiven and will still go to heaven. Then after church they go back to sinning again with no remorse. That makes no sense to me. Why would horrible people still get to go to heaven? Cause they believe in Jesus? And what about good people that don't believe in Jesus? They going to hell? That sounds like some bullshit to me."

"So you don't believe in God at all?" I asked.

"If He or she exists, I don't know anything about them. They say God is good, but if so, why does so much bad happen in this world? The church is supposed to be this *light* that guides people, but they're not. Church folk call themselves sheep but there's a lot of wolves in sheep's clothing. They judge you, gossip about you, and through all the sermons, you learn more about money then you do about God."

I didn't know about God either. My parents didn't believe in God at all. We didn't go to church and they typically looked down on anyone who did. They thought church people were simple fools being bamboozled by a system that was only trying to take their money and leave them oppressed and obedient. The only thing my parents believed in was hard work and honor. They wanted me to work hard to get good grades and a good job. They wanted me to honor them by obeying them, not getting pregnant and not using drugs. They were care-free hippie liberals in the world, but with me, they were strict oppressive bureaucrats. My education was their main priority. If I made any grade less than an A, I was grounded for weeks.

Chapter 2 – Erica in June 1995

"Mom, please can I go? You don't have to pay for anything," I begged my mom to let me spend the weekend with Lovey and her family at Virginia Beach. They usually went every summer and that year, they invited me.

"That's just it, I don't want you to be a burden on them."

"It won't be a burden Ms. Decker. My parents want her to come and keep me occupied. Please can she go? You'd be doing us a favor," Lovey cosigned.

"Well let me just give Charles and Dianne a call and make sure it's okay."

Lovey and I held hands, quietly pleaded, and anxiously waited as my mom called her parents and chatted. When she hung up the phone, she looked at me, then Lovey, then me again.

"Oh, all right," she spoke. "You can go."

"Yaaaay! Virginia Beach, Virginia Beach!" we chanted in unison.

It would be my first time seeing the ocean. I was so excited. I packed everything in my bag. Three swimming suits, five outfits, flip flops, tennis shoes, dress shoes, books, magazines, sunscreen, and the most important item, my game boy.

"Whoa, whoa whoa. Are you moving out? Just thought you were going for a weekend," my mom teased.

"I just want to be prepared for anything. I don't know if they are going to go to church, so I had to pack church clothes. I packed dress clothes in case they wanted to go out to a fancy restaurant. I need a different swimsuit for each day. Lovey likes to work out, so I need exercise gear."

"Wow!" my mom said as she looked through my stuff, "you did forget one thing…underwear."

"Oh crap!"

I ran back to my room and grabbed seven pairs, just in case, then hurried back passing the kitchen on the way. Eddie, my mom's boyfriend of a whopping three months was walking around the kitchen wearing only shorts and looking for something to eat. He waived to me and I rolled my eyes knowing that he had spent the night. He was the third guy to spend the night at our house that year. I hid my underwear under my shirt as I walked past him nd then I quickly stuffed them in my bag. Lovey knocked on my door right on time.

"Bye mom!" I yelled as I rushed out the door.

"Wait! Where's my kiss?"

"Huh," I sighed then back tracked to plant a wet sloppy strawberry on her cheek.

She laughed, "Love you Hun! Have fun! Be safe! Make good choices!"

"Yeah, yeah yeah," I responded as I ran with Lovey to her parent's car.

We climbed in the back where her grandmother Mrs. Mae greeted me with a smile. I never knew my grandparents. They died before I was born. But Ms. Mae I've known since I met Lovey. She always treated me kindly. She gave me hugs and kisses whenever she saw me, called me her adopted granddaughter, and she even sent me gifts for Christmas. She was the closest thing I knew to a grandparent and I was glad she was accompanying us. She offered me her famous homemade chocolate chip cookies, a snack she packed for the trip. They were my favorite dessert so I gladly accepted.

"Virginia Beach, Virginia Beach!" Lovey and I chanted, excited about our upcoming adventures.

Mrs. Mae laughed and joined in with our ranting, further annoying Lovey's parents. The drive was longer than need be because traffic on Friday afternoon leaving the city was monstrous. But Lovey and I didn't care. We enjoyed playing road trip games and talking about everything.

"Punch buggy no punch back!" I said as I punched her in the arm.

"Ow, jerk."

I laughed. "So, when I am 25, I want to get married and have three kids. I'm going to name them Ryu, Cammy, and Bison."

"Bison? Ryu? What kind of names are those?" she asked.

"You know, Street Fighter. I love that movie."

"Oh, my parents won't let me watch stuff like that. Plus, we don't have cable. They think it will warp my brain." Lovey jokingly waived her fingers at me like she was trying to extract my brain waves.

I shook my head. "So, what about you? What are you going to name your kids?"

"If it's a girl, I want to name her Jasmine. And if it's a boy, Jordan," she announced.

"Jordan could be a boy or a girl's name. Why don't you name it Jordan either way?"

"Cause, I like Jordan for a boy but not for a girl."

"We're here!" Dianne announced.

"Yay!" we said.

We jumped out the car, grabbed our bags, and rushed to the hotel hoping we could quickly change into our bathing suits and get on the beach. The hotel was two blocks away from the beach. We could see the beautiful waves from the balcony of our hotel room. Seagulls flew overhead. People walked, jogged, or road bikes along the boardwalk. We noticed the storm clouds forming over the ocean, but we hoped the rain would hold off for a few hours. It didn't. As soon as we got our swimsuits on, thunder and lightning invaded our vacation plans. The storm lasted all of Friday night and Saturday day. We kept ourselves busy running around the hotel room, playing Gameboy, and watching movies. Normally Lovey's parents restricted her use of electronics but because we were on vacation, they were more lenient.

Then on Sunday, the sun came out. It was a bright beautiful day with not a cloud in sight. We got up with the sunrise, jumped into our swimsuits and rushed Lovey's parents out the door with all our beach gear. Mrs. Mae's arthritis was acting up so she decided to admire us from the hotel balcony.

Dianne and Charles picked a spot to set up while Lovey and I ripped off our t-shirts, kicked off our flip flops, and ran to the water. We jumped over waves, frolicked, danced, and dove. I scratched my neck then beckoned Lovey to watch as I preformed what I thought was a super straight perfectly vertical handstand in the water. She laughed as I flopped my legs then fell sideways. When I came up, I saw Lovey scratching under her arm. Then she jumped up yelling "underwater tea party." She went under the water and sat on the bottom of the ocean pretending to sip tea and talk. I dove down with her but couldn't stay down for too long. Not only was I not great at holding my breath, but I also always floated to the surface. My butt stayed up out of the water as I tried to keep my head under and participate in Lovey's tea party.

When I came up gasping for air. I noticed my butt feeling quite uncomfortable. I scratched it then scratched an itch on the top of my head. I looked over and Lovey was scratching her head too.

"Lovey, are you itchy?" I asked.

"Yeah," she responded as she continued to scratch more intensely.

"Me too."

The itch was getting more severe and covered my entire body. I was scratching my arms, my leg, and under my developing breast. I wanted to scratch my privates, but I knew how inappropriate that would look. I looked, but there was no rash on my arms. There were no jelly fish around. We hadn't had breakfast yet, so it wasn't something we ate.

"It's the water!" Lovey and I both realized together. We ran out of that water and over to Dianne and Charles itching and scratching the whole way.

"There's something in the water. It's making us itch," Lovey announced.

"There should be some showers along the boardwalk somewhere. Go walk until you find one and rinse off," Dianne recommended.

We took off for the boardwalk and made a left thinking that was our best bet to find a shower. We walked along the boardwalk wiggling with irritation the entire way. The more we walked the more it itched, and the more we scratched. There was no shower in sight.

"Where's the shower!" I yelled.

"I don't know. It's crazy. There's usually one every few blocks. But I haven't seen one and we've walked a mile at least."

Then I saw it, a couple of blocks ahead. The outdoor shower was surrounded by groups of people the majority of which were males of various ages.

"There's one!" I yelled as I high tailed it towards our saving grace.

The itch was so intense I wanted to rip my bathing suit off and scratch every part of me. When we got to the shower we impatiently waited our turn. We stood there hopping from one foot to the other trying not to itch. There was a little boy and his mom that went before us. They took forever trying to rinse every little speck of sand off their bodies. When they left, we ran under the shower head almost pushing them out the way. I pulled down the lever and the most refreshing water poured out.

"Ahhhhhhhhhhhhhh," we both said in unison.

Onlookers twisted their heads to the side as they heard our pleasurable moans and watched us shower like a scene from *Flashdance*.

"God, oh yes! Yes!" I said as I pulled my bikini bottoms forward allowing water to drip down below. I didn't care who watched. I just had to get whatever was in that water off of me.

"Oh yeah! Right there. That's the spot," Lovey shouted as she pulled the front top of her swimsuit forward allowing water to drip on her breast buds. We could have stayed under that water for hours, but we had to let other itchy people get in there too.

"Sea lice," a nice older woman with a heavy southern accent spoke as we walked away.

"Huh?"

"Sea lice. They are small ocean creatures that come out after a big storm and cause you to itch. Don't worry. They are harmless. Just irritating."

We decided to spend the rest of our day playing in the sand. Storms and sea lice ruined our weekend; nevertheless, it was the best weekend of my entire childhood. Unfortunately, it was the last weekend of my childhood too. It seemed like as soon as we returned, we were hit with bad news.

A week later my mom entered my room. "Erica, can I talk to you for a minute?" I let out a deep sigh, annoyed that she was interrupting my Saturday morning cartoons. I turned off the television and sat up. "Erica, I have some bad news. Mrs. Mae passed away in her sleep last night."

"Passed away? What do you mean passed away? I just saw her. We just…"

"I know it's hard to understand, but Mrs. Mae is no longer with us. The Good Lord has called her home."

"But…I don't want her to go. I need her and…"

"Erica, Lovey needs you right now. Maybe you should go over and be with her."

"Can you come with me?"

"I have to go to work." I dropped my head. I really didn't think I could handle it alone. My mom noticed my resistance and said, "I tell you what, I'll have Eddie go with you instead."

"Eddie? But he's…"

"Eddie is a good guy. He's going to be your stepfather one day so maybe you should get to know him a little better."

Learning that Mrs. Mae had died was heavy on a Saturday morning, but learning I was going to have a stepfather soon weighted me down even more. Both reports filled me with so many emotions. *Death. What is death? What is life? Why would a good God allow Mrs. Mae to die? Stepfather. What would that be like? Lovey had a great dad. Would it be like that? That would be nice. Maybe I should accept Eddie.*

I went along, allowing Eddie to accompany me to Lovey's house. Lovey was a mess. When I walked in her room I found her laying on her bed crying unconsolably. There were no words I could say to ease the pain. I didn't even try. I hopped in the bed and held her until she fell asleep.

After, Eddie took me to get ice cream.

"You are a great friend to Lovey," he said over banana splits. "I'm proud of you. She needed you and you were there."

I smiled, chocolate staining my teeth. He giggled.

"So, your mom told you I was going to marry her soon, huh?"

"Yeah, are you?"

"I plan on it. That would make me your stepdad and would make me responsible for you. So, anything you need – clothes, shoes, protection. I got you."

I nodded my head, feeling special, safe, and cared for. *Maybe life is turning around for me and my mom.* "I'll take that car," I joked, pointing to his '91 Mustang. I loved his car; she was a beauty. I wanted to grow up and drive one just like it.

Eddie laughed, "You're cute, but you're not getting my car. I'll teach you how to drive it though."

"Drive? I'm not old enough to drive. My mom would kill me if I tried."

"Don't worry about your mom. What she doesn't know won't hurt her. It could be our little secret," Eddie said as he brushed a lock of hair out of my face.

I smiled and nodded in agreement, eager to learn adult tasks before my time.

Chapter 3 – Erica in December 1995

"Fight, fight, fight!" I heard my classmates chanting as I threw blows at Lovey's head and she threw blows back. A crowd gathered around us as we rumbled. I was so mad at her for ratting me out to my teacher. She was such a goodie-two-shoes. She could never tell a lie and she folded quickly under even a little bit of pressure. If she had just kept her mouth shut, Mrs. Anderson would never have known I plagiarized my paper. Lovey was a grade above me, and she had Mrs. Anderson for seventh grade English last year. I didn't think Mrs. Anderson would remember Lovey's paper. She was an old crabby senile woman. Plus, I changed a bunch of words to make it my own. But as soon as I saw Lovey walking out of the principal's office I knew she had been interrogated about the paper and had probably confessed everything.

I hated Lovey. She always got everything she wanted, and I never got anything. Both her parents were still together. They were kind, smart, and rich. Lovey never went hungry. She never wanted for anything. She always had the best clothes, the best shoes, and the best toys. Lovey's mom took her to get her hair done every two weeks. Plus, Lovey was beautiful. She was thin, cream-complexioned, with loose curly hair. All the boys drooled when she walked by. Lovey did not know my pain. She did not know my secret. She lived carefree while I was haunted.

The principal spoke of how disappointed she was in me and then punished me with a two-day suspension. I was waiting for my mom in the front office when I saw Lovey walk past. She looked at me with inquisitive concern. Rage filled my heart and clouded my vision. I didn't care about anything but causing her as much pain as I felt. I walked right out of the office and punched her square in the face.

Lovey had never been in a fight before though I had been in plenty. I underestimated her strength. When she hit back it hurt. I felt a punch in the right eye followed by two quick upper cuts to the left chin. I stumbled backward but caught my balance quickly, knowing that if I fell, she could easily stomp me and dominate the altercation. I couldn't let that happen. Anyone in that school who got beat down would be forever a target of ridicule and abuse.

I lunged at Lovey, wrapping my hands around her neck. We both fell onto the floor and rolled around continuing to punch and grab each other until I felt the tug of a large man lift me up. I continued to kick and scratch at the air.

"Calm down!" Mr. Bunch, the vice principal said as he held me. Lovey got up on her own. She didn't try to continue to fight. Aside from her heavy breathing, she stood still, looking shocked and dismayed.

We both ended up sitting in the principal's office in yellow chairs on opposite sides of the room.

"What has gotten into you two? You are best friends," Principal Ware said from behind her desk.

Neither of us answered.

Mr. Bunch stood with his arms folded looking at both of us. He was ready to intervene in case more violence erupted. Lovey started crying profusely. I was not fazed by the theatrics. I rolled my eyes and slouched in the chair with my arms folded across my chest.

"Erica, I'm increasing your suspension to four days! Lovey! We will talk when your mom gets here."

It didn't surprise me that Lovey would get by with just a slap on the wrist while I got increased suspension. Lovey got away with everything.

Lovey's mom arrived before mine. She didn't yell at Lovey. She gave her a big hug and said, "Oh Lovey, are you alright?" Lovey tried to respond but was crying too hysterically to make sense.

"Huh…mom…huh…sorry…I…annnnnn nh."

"It's okay honey. Come, let's get you home."

And they left. No beatings. No yelling. No punishment. They just left. But when my mom came it was a different story.

"Erica, what have you done now? You know I work way too hard to be coming down to this school to talk with the principal about your ignorant behavior," she yelled as she slapped me on the back of the head. "Four days! Four days! What am I supposed to do with you for four days?"

"I can stay home by myself. I'm old enough now."

"Oh, so you grown now? Grown folks don't get into fist fights with their best friends. And you expect me to let you stay home watching TV and getting into trouble? Ha! I think not. This is not a vacation. This is a punishment and will be handled accordingly."

My mom kept to her word. She took away my computer, video games, television, radio, and phone privileges. She got me textbooks about psychology and spirituality then forced me to read them as I sat in a cubical at her office while she worked. The books were boring. It was like reading 500 pages of an instruction manual. If she caught me nodding off she'd bang hard on the desk to wake me up. It was pure torture. But I survived and after, I was back in school.

I saw Lovey walking down the hallway with Eva and Shantel, two of the most popular girls at our school. They were laughing and joking as if they had been friends all school year. When they saw me they both said, "Ew." Eva looked me up and down then said to Lovey, "Girl, we'll check you later, alright?"

"Alright," Lovey spoke freely then she approached me. "Hey," she whispered.

"What's up," I said back and gave her a head nod. I tried to play it cool, but truthfully, I missed her dearly and I regretted everything. I hated that she sold me out and I hated that her life was so much better than mine. But I loved her. She was the sweetest person I knew. She was indeed my best friend and one of the few real friends I had. But I didn't want to show my enthusiasm in seeing her again. I didn't want to admit I was wrong and apologize, so I planned to keep my distance.

"I missed you so much!" she said as she wrapped her arms around me giving me a big bear hug. My heart melted and my plans of cool social distancing went to shit.

"I missed you too!" I said as we both started sobbing.

"I'm soooo sorrrrryyyyy," we both cried.

The cries turned into laughter as we realized how silly we were being. We wiped our tears away and went back to life as if nothing had ever happened. But something did happen. It happened to me, and as a result my life would never be the same. I wish I had told her then. But I couldn't. I was too afraid.

Chapter 4 – Trey

I remember the first time I saw Lovey. It was the first day of third grade and my first day at a new school. My family had moved to D.C. from Georgia just a few weeks prior. I was nervous the entire day. My mom had signed me up to participate in an afterschool program. She worked long hours and was unable to pick me up directly after school. I hated it. I felt I was old enough to walk home by myself and stay there until she got home. But my mom was not having it. My teacher escorted me to the gym where the afterschool program students met. I sat pouting on the bleachers when Lovey walked in and time slowed down.

She was a pretty little thing just one year younger than I was. Her hair was long and braided in two. She smiled at me, winked, and sat a few tiers up from me. Her best friend Erica sat next to her. They were laughing, talking, and joking. I kept my gaze forward but listened intently to their conversation, wondering if they'd mention me, the handsome new kid. They didn't.

But on the playground the next day Erica approached me. She introduced herself and Lovey. She said that she recognized me from around the neighborhood. Apparently, she and her mom drove past my house while we were unpacking the moving truck. She only lived two blocks away from me and Lovey around the corner. After that, Erica, Lovey, and I were inseparable like The Three Musketeers. We had so much fun together. After school and on weekends we were always at one of our houses joking around, playing video games, or outside running around the neighborhood. In the summer we were always at the local pool or at the playground just being our silly selves.

We grew apart a little when I went to middle school. I met male friends and formed a clique with them. But I was still cool with Lovey and Erica. Erica matured physically a lot faster than Lovey did. She started developing breasts and hips at age eleven. My attention quickly switched from Lovey to Erica as soon as my male friends pointed out her endowment.

I was a late bloomer, the shortest and skinniest in my middle school clique. My homeboys on the other hand were tall, muscular and athletic. Erica flirted with them and ignored me. She didn't see me as a lover. She treated me like I was her annoying little brother even though I was two years older. I made it noticeably clear that I wanted her. She ignored me and kept trying to pass me off to Lovey.

Lovey didn't start filling out until well after her fourteenth birthday. Her parents sent her to a private school while Erica and I stayed in the public sector. But I remember Lovey walking home from school in her short Catholic school skirt and button up sweater. A school uniform never looked so good. I often fantasized about ripping off her clothes and screwing her all night. But she never even hinted that I had any shot. I kept my distance, only platonically engaging with her.

The summer after I turned 16, Erica showed up at my house alone while my mom was at work.

"Hey Erica, where's Lovey?" Rarely did you see one without the other.

"She's doing a summer science and arts program at University of Maryland. You know how her smart ass is. She's already thinking about her career. I'm just trying to get through high school."

I didn't expect to lose my virginity that day, but I didn't oppose it when it happened. We started off innocent, just watching television and eating cereal. Then Erica started to kiss me. She kissed my neck and started stroking my penis. All I could think was, *Is this really happening? Am I finally getting my first piece of ass?* I had waited for that moment seemingly forever. All my friends were sleeping around with plenty of women, and I had to listen to their stories about who was tight, who was loose, how good whoever was, and who they never called back after fucking. I had no stories. I'd just shake my head and pretended like I understood what they were talking about when in fact I had no idea. I liked Lovey, but I wanted to have sex. I didn't care with whom.

Erica whipped out a condom and I thought my head was going to explode. I was so nervous. I had no idea what I was doing. I didn't want Erica, who was very experienced, to joke about me or to say I sucked in bed. I fumbled with that condom while Erica sat there looking annoyed. She took the condom from me, ripped it open and put it on me. Then she hopped on top of me and started riding. She felt so good inside. Warm and wet. I didn't last long. I grabbed her ass tight and let out a huge roar when I orgasmed. She smiled at me then hopped off, used a tissue to wipe herself, then she got dressed and left.

I laid on the couch dazed. I wasn't a virgin anymore. I didn't feel special or different. There was no enlightenment. I didn't feel more accomplished or more mature. In fact, I felt more like a man before the encounter than I did after. After, I felt used, lonely, and I worried about what Erica would say about me. Would she tell everyone I was a minute man? Or that I didn't know what I was doing? Would all my friends joke and laugh at my incompetence?

The summer went by without anyone mentioning, "Yo! I heard you fucked Erica." That was a relief. When I saw Erica again she didn't mention it – also a relief. She didn't come back for seconds though – a disappointment. She did not look at me with lust nor disgust. She proceeded with life like nothing ever happened. And I followed her lead.

Sixteen was a good year for me. After Erica came Keisha, Monique, Natalie, Maria, and Janet. I didn't have to work hard for any of them. I'd just ask them if they wanted to hang out. Some of them I was fucking on the first date. Others, it took a few weeks before they let me hit. They were all pretty girls, but they all had different personalities and goals. Some wanted relationships, but I wasn't feeling that. Some just wanted to fuck which was a lot more appealing to me. I never mislead anyone. I'd simply let them know that I didn't want a relationship and if they wanted one, I'd stop calling them. It was no big deal to me.

I learned a lot from those ladies. They taught me what to say, what to do, and where to touch to get their motors running. By Christmas, I was an experienced lover and that got me even more play.

But Lovey, she was a safe I could not crack. We hung out all the time and I'd often drop little hints that I wanted her, but she never took the bait. I respected that, but her resistance made me want her even more.

On my 17th birthday my mom surprised me with a 1994 Toyota Camry, and I was the envy of the neighborhood. Even Lovey started to make side eyes at me. When she kissed me in the club, I was overwhelmed by the butterflies I felt in my heart. I was ready and willing to give up my playboy ways to be her one and only. She told me that she'd call me the next day and I was hoping that it would be the start of our friendship changing into a romantic relationship. But she didn't call. The day after, I still didn't hear from her. When two more days went by with no phone call I decided to call her. She didn't answer.

After school the next day I ran to the metro station picking up a flower from someone's garden on the way there. I sat on top of a newspaper stand and waited for her to get off the train. She walked through the gates with a book bag strapped to her back and a few extra books held in her arms.

"Lovey!" I called out as I saw her. She turned around looking confused. When she saw it was me calling her she smiled. Her smile warmed me.

"Trey, what are you doing here?"

"I figured I'd walk you home from school," I said as I handed her the flower.

She took it, smelled it, and smiled even harder. "Where'd you get this from?"

"Oh, I got it for you."

"Thanks." She turned and we started walking the five blocks to her house.

"Man, it's foggy out…creepy."

She smiled, "I like the fog. It feels like I'm walking in a cloud."

I loved that Lovey saw the beauty in things most of us found strange.

That was the start of my official courtship. Every day I repeated the cycle. I waited for her at the metro each day with a different flower in my hand and carried her books as I walked her home. Along the way we'd talk about everything. She opened up to me and talked about the friends and foes she made at her school. She talked of her teachers, her classes, and her dreams. She loved to dance, she loved science, and she loved art. She shared with me the masterpieces that she scribbled throughout her school notebooks. They were beautiful. She had skills and I was sure her talents were a set up for a bright future. She wanted to be an architect and I knew she'd be a great one. I loved listening to her. I loved her stories and her drive.

I enjoyed sharing my life's stories with her too. I didn't know what I wanted to be or what I liked. I figured I'd go to college and figure it out then. I talked a lot about my family, and I never did that with anyone. My father was a drug dealer and was murdered by a rival. My mother feared the people who killed him would come after us. That was why we moved to DC. Lovey was the only person I felt comfortable sharing that with. She was understanding. She listened attentively and never passed judgement on me or my family.

After two weeks of daily walking and talking, she kissed me on the cheek then turned to walk into her house. In those two weeks, that was the most affection I had been offered so I thought it my duty to make the next move. I grabbed her arm before she could leave my presence and I leaned in to kiss her. She rejected me. She turned her head and held up her hand. My lips landed on the palm of her hand instead of on her mouth like I had hoped.

"For real? It's like that?" I asked. Lovey was silent. "Look Lovey, I like you, like a lot. I want you. And I know you want me too. So, what's up?"

"Nothing's up. I'm just not down for you like that."

"What about that night in the club? You were down for me then. Then you went back cold again. No phone calls. No nothing. Why?"

She sighed and rolled her eyes. "I know you slept with Erica."

My whole world seemed to collapse on me. I was speechless. When I lost my virginity I didn't think it would affect my chances of getting the person I really wanted.

"Mmmm, hmmm," she said as she walked away.

I tried to put together a sentence, but my words came out all jumbled. I had blown it. My chance with Lovey was a failure before it even started. I walked home feeling defeated. I didn't show up to meet her at the metro station the next day. I wanted to, but I had no idea what I would say to her. I sat in my room trying to concentrate on my homework when I heard a knock at the door. I ran downstairs and opened the door. To my surprise, Lovey stood in the entryway with a flower in her hand.

"Lovey? What are you doing here?"

"Did you forget about our walk date?"

"I thought…I…you…"

She smiled and handed me the flower, "May I come in?"

"Uh, sure."

I stepped out of the way and let her enter. I closed the door behind me and immediately we started kissing. I grabbed her ass and hoisted her up on the entryway table. I ripped off that cute school-girl sweater. Buttons flew everywhere. She wrapped her legs around my waist and continued to wrestle my tongue with her own. My dick got rock hard as my pelvis grinded against hers. I could feel how warm and wet she was through her panties. I grabbed her thighs with both hands and inched my way up under her skirt. I grabbed her panties and started to take them down.

"Whoa, wait," she stopped me.

Fuuuuucccckkkkk! I was so close!

"I'm a virgin," she looked nervous as she said it.

"I'll be gentle." I leaned in to kiss her again.

"Nope, I can't. Not like this. I'm sorry." She got up to leave.

"Wait, Lovey. Don't go. We don't have to have sex. Just let me hold you and kiss you."

She turned to me and started kissing me again. I lead her to my couch and passionately kissed her back. I was gentle with her as I inched my hand up her shirt and started to caress her nipple. The moans she uttered at my touch excited me even more. My dick was rock hard and ready to feel her insides. I thought I was going to explode.

"Can I taste you?" I whispered in her ear. She clamped up and looked at me inquisitively. I could tell she was pondering the idea. "We don't have to do anything further than that. I just want to taste you. That's all."

She nodded. I kissed her cheek, her neck, then completed my path of gentle kisses to her inner thigh. Her legs started to tremble – excitement, nervousness, and pleasure combined. I slipped off her lace panties and lifted her skirt. I rubbed my thumb across her clit and could feel her heat radiating as I traced my finger around the ring of her opening. Her breathing quickened.

I kissed her pleasure zone, tasting all her juices. She purred like a kitten as I slipped my tongue in and out of her tight abyss. I wanted to claim her as mine, so I gently penetrated her with my finger and massaged her inside. I grabbed my penis with the other hand and began to stroke myself wishing that my hand were her walls. I trace my name across her voluptuous clitoris with my tongue. T, I traced as she exhaled with pleasure. R, her volume rose. E, she grabbed my head and arched her back. Y, she shrieked. I felt her walls clench up then start to pulsate - her vibrations teasing my tongue. Sweet nectar squirted and started pooling on the couch. I wanted to slurp up every drop. She was so delicious I could barely contain myself. I became drunk off her wine and high with her pleasure.

Her heavy breathing started to slow as I douched her inner thigh with kisses. My heart filled with pride knowing I was responsible for her first orgasm.

"That was tasty," I smiled deviously at her.

"Yes, it was," she stated, still intoxicated from my tongue lashing. "Umm, sorry about the couch." She blushed, embarrassed about the mess she'd made.

"Don't worry about it. I'm just glad you gave me the opportunity to please you. Maybe next time you could please me too."

She smiled, kissed me, then left. But her smell lingered and teased my senses. My hand was still saturated with her juice. I used it as lubrication while I stroked myself. I recollected her taste, her moans, and her pulsations. I fantasized that she was riding me, licking me, and loving me. When I reached my climax, I shouted her name - my creamy liquids mixing with hers on my hand. I laid there satisfied in knowing I was getting closer to my goal with Lovey. Soon I'd be stroking her insides and making her call my name.

Chapter 5 – Lovey in October 1998

"So, your homework for this weekend," Mr. Harmon said, "is to take a picture that makes a powerful political statement. We will develop them Monday and take turns sharing our pictures and discussing the statements the pictures make."

He was speaking to the entire class but the only one who seemed interested was me. I loved my photography class, and I was glad my school offered it. I had no interest in politics. I would rather have done pictures depicting beautiful architecture, but as long as I was behind the camera or in the darkroom, I was pleased.

I anticipated Trey would be waiting at the metro station to walk me home and was disappointed when I didn't see him. I hoped he wasn't running away after the event we had the day before. I had never experienced anything like it before. I had no idea that a man's tongue could make me soak a couch.

"Hey Squirt!" I heard Trey's voice call from behind me. I turned around and saw him running after me with a long-stemmed red rose in his hand.

"Trey!" I was blushing though I tried to hide my excitement. "You're late. And why are you calling me Squirt?"

"I had to run to the grocery store to buy you this." He handed me the flower. "And, you know why I called you Squirt," he teased.

He pulled me close to him and kissed my neck. That kiss sent shivers down my spine. I could feel me getting wet all over again though I tried to ignore the impulse.

"It's beautiful." I kissed him on the cheek.

"That's all I get? After yesterday?"

I smiled, then gave him a long, sweet, seductive kiss on the lips.

"That's my girl."

We walked to my house hand in hand and chatted about our day.

"You want to come in?" I asked when we stepped on my porch.

"You know I do, but my mom's getting off her shift early today. You know she'll have my ass if I'm not there when she gets home."

We kissed again then went our separate ways.

I called Erica as soon as I got in and asked for some suggestions regarding the photography project. She was way more into politics than I. She was headstrong and bold. She wasn't sure what she wanted to be when she grew up, but I always thought she'd make a great lawyer or politician one day.

"Mr. Harmon wants me to make a political statement with my pictures. I have no idea where to start."

"Girl, we live in DC. You don't get more political than that. How 'bout we go downtown tomorrow. I'm sure we will have plenty of material to work with down there."

"Cool, see you tomorrow."

"Cool."

The next morning I loaded my camera with film and we headed to the metro station. During the ride I told her about my heated encounter with Trey. "So, um, something happened on Thursday."

"Mmm, hmmm," she inched closer to listen to the juicy details.

"Something happened with Trey."

"Huh, you little slut. You let him hit. Didn't you?" she playfully joked but she was loud enough to catch the attention of surrounding patrons who scooted away, gave us the side eye, and held their newspapers closer to their faces.

"Shhhh. No, I didn't…But I let him eat me out."

"Damn girl. You got him like that? So, how was it?"

"It was good. I soaked his couch. And squirted."

"Dang, for real? Like porn star squirt?"

"Shhhh, girl yes. Damn, why you gotta be so loud?"

"Mmmm, I've never done no shit like that before. Hmmm, maybe I'll try to get Antonio's big ass dick to make me squirt."

"Antonio? You mean Antonio Hightower? Who we went to elementary school with?"

"Yep, that's the one. But he is all grown up now. We talk every now and then."

"And by talk, you mean fuck."

She smiled.

"Next stop, Smithsonian," the conductor announced over the loudspeaker.

"Oh, that's our stop!"

I'd visited The National Mall a million times, but I still marveled at the beauty of the museums and monuments. The architecture and design of the place was the reason I wanted to be an architect in the first place. I took pictures of everything – the escalator ascending from the dark tunnels of the metro to the open airy outdoors, the pigeons that nibbled on crumbs tourist left behind, the American flags surrounding the Washington monument as they blew in the wind, a bottle of Heineken shattered on the sidewalk. It was all inspirational and had meaning, but I hadn't found the prominent political shot I was looking for.

"Hey, let's go in there!" Erica suggested.

"The National Museum of American History?"

"Yeah, it's my favorite."

"I know. I've been in there with you hundreds of times. I doubt I find a powerful photo op in there though."

"You might."

I rolled my eyes.

"Oh, come on!" Erica said as she grabbed my arm and pulled me along.

We first went to an exhibit featuring the gowns of the First Ladies. We strolled along browsing the beautiful dresses once worn by the wives of past presidents. As we stopped to gaze at Jackie Kennedy's white sleeveless gown a voice rang out behind us.

"You know Jacqueline Kennedy was not only a fashion icon of the 60s, she was an incredibly talented reporter, photographer, and editor. She was also fluent in Spanish, Italian and French which proved useful for her husband's foreign travels and policies."

Erica and I both turned around and faced a tall and thin caramel-complexioned guy with Clark Kent vibes. His hair was clean cut. He wore a burgundy polo shirt and navy-blue slacks. His Smithsonian employee name tag was crookedly pinned on his right breast pocket. He adjusted his glasses as he spoke. There was a handsome face underlying his geek appeal and the three of us awkwardly stood in silence after he finished the unexpected history lesson. Erica and I smiled, gave him a head nod, then walked away.

We browsed a few more exhibits and when we came to Dorothy's ruby slippers from *The Wizard of Oz* I felt a nerdy presence on my right.

"You know, originally the slippers were not red. They were silver. MGM changed them for the movie because they wanted to showcase their new color cinematography."

I rolled my eyes and ignored him, but Erica entertained. She leaned over me to flirt with him directly.

"Really, that's so interesting. Tell me more, Handsome."

"Did you know that the Tin Man's son married Dorothy's daughter thirty-five years after the film was produced?"

I quietly slipped out from between them allowing them to continue their provocative charade. I took a few pictures of Archie Bunker's chair from *All in the Family* while I quietly reflected on the social conflicts the show addressed. *Maybe I can make that my political statement,* I thought. I was enjoying my moment of solitude when *Kent* and Erica invaded my space with their deep discussions and shallow giggles.

"*All in the Family* shed life on the ridiculousness of conservative ideas and racism through comedy."

Annoyed at the interruption I answered, "Yes, I know."

"Yes," he adjusted his glasses. "It is such a classic American concept, but did you know it was based on a British show?"

"Geesh, I had no idea," I sarcastically spoke. Erica rolled her eyes at me. She was clearly trying to take off *Kent's* glasses and get her a piece of his superman.

"So, what's your name History Boy?" she asked.

"Jerome."

"Oh, Jerome's in the house! Jerome's in the ha ha ha house!"

"I hate that Martin used my name for such a silly character," Jerome huffed.

I acknowledged his validity, "Jerome, after Saint Jerome the patron saint of librarians. That suits you much better."

He blushed as he stared at me. "Exactly," he said.

I smiled and stared back, noticing his charm for the first time.

"So, you've been following us around the whole time we've been here. Are you gonna ask one of us out or something?" Erica boldly asked.

He nervously scratched his head, "Uh."

"Oh, I'll make it easy for you." She pointed to me. "That one has a boyfriend."

"I don't have a boyfriend," I contested.

"Uh, Trey."

"He's not my boyfriend."

"Oh, yeah, he's just someone whose mouth you squirt in every now and then."

"See, that's why I never tell you anything! I share a little and the next thing I know my business is all over the neighborhood."

"It's just Jerome! He doesn't know anyone in our neighborhood. Who is he going to tell?"

She batted her eyes. I rolled mine.

"Um, okay. That's interesting," Jerome interrupted. "So, Erica. Can I get your number and maybe call you sometime?"

"I thought you'd never ask," she smiled as she whipped out a pen and jotted down her number.

"He was kinda cute," Erica said, draping her arm over me as we walked out of the building.

"Yeah, he was alright."

Sitting propped up against the wall of the museum was a homeless man holding a sign that said, "Homeless Vet, please spare some change." Wealthy people with Gucci bags and Louboutin shoes walked past like he was invisible. I adjusted the focus on my camera and started to shoot.

"Am I blocking your shot?" he asked.

"You are my shot."

"Really?" He straightened and smiled. "I feel special."

"So, what's your story?" Erica asked.

"My story?"

"Yeah, how did you, a veteran at that, end up, uh…"

"Homeless?"

"Yeah."

"Well, I did serve this country - the Vietnam War - and I wasn't even drafted. My dumb ass volunteered to go. Thought my country needed me. Thought I'd be a war hero, be someone my son could look up to. Know what I mean? But even as a vet, a Black man still don't get no respect. I got injured my second tour - still got some scrap metal in me. It caused me a lotta pain and the doctors shot me all up with Morphine to help. After a while, that shit stopped working. I took stronger stuff just to get a little relief. Spent all I had trying to numb my pain. I lost my family, my friends, and that's that. But God is good. A lot of my friends didn't make it. But I'm still here."

"Damn, that shit sucks," Erica said.

I slipped a twenty in his cup.

"Thank you. God Bless."

"Uh, huh," I responded, then turned and walked away. *How can someone with such a shitty life still believe in God and believe He is good? Must have been the drugs.*

"Damn girl. Why you give him that? You know he just gonna spend it on drugs."

I shrugged. I knew Erica was right. I should have given him a meal instead of money. But I hoped he would use at least some of that money to get something to eat. On the way home I thought about how I would present the picture. First, I had to think of a title - *The Vet, The Fight of Our Country, Privileged.* I wasn't sure, but the statement was clear. This man fought and nearly died for our freedom. He served this country so that we can go on living a privileged life with our fortunate jobs and our luxurious clothes. The same people he fought for now pass him by refusing to help or even acknowledge his sacrifice.

When I walked into my house my mom greeted me at the door.

"How was the photo shoot?"

"It was good," I responded. I tended to be short with my mom. I hated having her in my business. She always had an unwelcomed opinion about my life that she was not shy with sharing.

"You went with Erica?"

"Yeah," I sighed. All I wanted to do was go upstairs to my room and watch television, but I had a feeling that a lecture was coming.

"You know, I'm not too sure about you hanging out with Erica. Seems like she is becoming a bad influence."

"Oh my God! Ma! Are you serious? Erica's been my friend since like forever and you want me to stop being her friend?"

"Well, yes. I know she's promiscuous. I see her running up and down the street with all them boys. Don't want her having an effect on you."

"Geesh! You always want to take everything from me. Now you want to take away my best friend. Dad! Please, can you talk some sense into your wife?"

"Hey! You are not going to disrespect me like that," Dianne scolded.

I rolled my eyes and whined, "Dad!"

My father was usually more reasonable, but less vocal. Unfortunately, with that dispute, he backed Diane. "Well, you know honey, your mom does have a point. Erica is…"

"Erica is a good person," I fussed. "She may be a little promiscuous…okay, a lot promiscuous, but she has a great heart, and I am not giving her up because you think she's a bad influence. I am making good grades and making good choices. She doesn't influence me. I influence her. I am not giving up the only person that makes me smile and laugh in this cruel world."

Chapter 6 – Trey in November 1998

Lovey was hooked. Every night since my tongue lashing she'd sneak me into her basement so we could spend the night together. She'd let me kiss her, touch her and lick her, but she always resisted me entering her. She'd give me a hand job at the end of each night to avoid back up. I was growing tired of the middle school affection. I wanted something more adult.

One of those nights when we were dry humping I tried to coax her into taking the next step. "Damn Squirt, you got me so high. Got me thinking about love and..."

"Hold up baby. You bout to make me...ohhh."

She vibrated beneath me then relaxed. I loved her post orgasm glow. Her laying there with a drunken smile on her face was adorable.

"Did you just say you love me?"

"You know I love you. We been friends since elementary. But uh..."

"You're not in love with me," she said rolling her eyes.

"I wasn't going to say that. I'm falling for you, hard. But I need more from you. I can't sleep. I can't eat. All I can think about is being inside you."

"You know I'm not ready for that yet."

"Look, we ain't got to have sex, but maybe you could…you know…give it a little kiss…suck it a little." She looked skeptical. "Come on girl. I do you every night. You gotta give me some love too. Look at him. Looking all sad and pitiful," I said, referencing my penis I'd pulled out of my pants. "He needs you." I was rock hard and yearning. "Please." I gave her my saddest puppy dog eyes.

"Oh, alright."

I couldn't hide my excitement when she leaned over and kissed the head with her plump lips. I let out a sigh. Then she licked it. I moaned. Then she took it in her mouth and started to scrape it with her teeth. "Ow girl, not so rough."

"Sorry, I never did this before."

She tried again, but it was even worse. More teeth scraping only slower and sloppier. She had no rhythm and she moved her back more than she moved her neck. She looked like a chicken trying to fly. To avoid discouraging her, I tried to fake like I was enjoying it. "Ohh, ah," *bite* "Ow!"

She looked at me concerned. I smiled and gave her the thumbs up. She proceeded with her uncoordinated chicken dance.

"Oh, alright, alright. That's good. Thank you, Squirt."

"That's it? You're done?"

"Yeah, I'm good."

"But I didn't make you cum."

"Oh, it's okay. I'd much rather kiss you instead."

She smiled and we continued to make out. But I was thoroughly disappointed. I needed me some pleasing and I was not getting anywhere with Lovey. Meanwhile, Keisha and Monique were continuously knocking at my door trying to rekindle. It took all I had to avoid their advances, but frustration with Lovey made them more tempting.

**

A few from my crew were in the locker room talking shit after gym class. Antonio was the loudmouth of the group. He was constantly bragging on his dick. I was half-assed listening to yet another story of him turning some girl out when he started getting into my business.

"Yo, you hit Lovey yet?"

I didn't want the other guys thinking I didn't have what it took to get any girl I wanted. But I didn't want to lie about Lovey either. "Nigga, you know I don't kiss and tell."

"Aw shit," the other fellows jokingly pumped me up.

"Mmm, whatever Nigga," Antonio called the bluff. "I know you ain't smash cause when I fucked her last week, her curves were still molded to my dick perfectly."

"What?" I stood up in disbelief. "What you say?" I was heated. I repeatedly balled up my fist trying to relieve the tension and rationalize. *He has to be playing. He's always joking around like that. Lovey's a virgin. She tight. But I mean, maybe she's not. Maybe she's been lying to me this whole time. Maybe that's why she hasn't slept with me yet. Maybe she doesn't want me to know she's lying.*

"Yo Antonio," Derrick said, seeing my anger building, "don't even play like that. You know that's Trey's girl. They been together forever."

Antonio laughed, "That's not his girl."

"Man Antonio, you so full of shit," I said, brushing him off. "You always lying on your dick. You ain't smashed half the girls you claim. You probably still a virgin."

"Oh, I'm lying?" He got in my face with a devious grin plastered on his face. "I know she squirt when she cum. How would I know that if I wasn't fucking her?"

I punched his face. He grabbed my arms and tried to take me down but I wiggled out of it and delivered three jabs to the left side of his face followed by a left hook and upper cut. He blocked my next punch and rammed his fist into my stomach knocking the wind out of me. I grabbed his ear and yanked his diamond stud out.

"Ow shit!" he screamed as blood dripped from the gash.

I kneed him in the groin and as he keeled over in pain, I delivered three more blows to the right side of his face then threw him into the lockers.

"Yo, break it up! Break it up!" The security guard came marching in and grabbed me, placing me in an arm restraint so I couldn't move. This gave Antonio the opportunity to get up and get in a cheap shot in before a second guard could restrain him. They escorted us both to the principal's office. I felt hurt, anger, and confusion as I reflected on the possibility that what he said was true. *How would he know she squirted if he wasn't with her? I didn't tell anyone. And as secretive as she is, I'm sure she didn't tell anyone either.*

Five days suspension was my punishment. I knew my mom would be disappointed. But I didn't care. I was filled with fury. *How could Lovey lie to me so easily? Plus, she was fucking Antonio's gump ass but not giving me any.*

I was at the metro station early that day. As soon as I saw Lovey come out the gate, I yelled to her, "Lovey!" She smiled when she saw me.

"You got something you need to tell me?"

Her countenance turned worried when she noticed my anger. "No, what?"

"Oh, so you ain't got nothing to tell me?"

"No! What's wrong?"

"How 'bout telling me about how you fucking Antonio."

"Antonio? Antonio Hightower?"

"Yeah, him."

She brushed me off. "I'm not fucking Antonio."

"See, I know you lying! Cause he know all about you, Squirt!"

She sucked her teeth, rolled her eyes and walked away. "You don't know what you're talking about."

"I know you ain't no virgin. You a ho just like the rest of them. Except you worse, you a lying ho!"

Her light face turned bright red. She approached me looking angrier than I felt. I didn't care. I wanted her to feel the pain she caused me. She slapped me then walked away. Her slap stung my pride more than my face. Onlookers pointed, snickered, and stared which added insult to injuries. I grew more heated – desiring to grab Lovey by the back of her neck, turn her around, and tell her a few things about herself. Instead, I walked away and vowed never to talk to her again.

"I don't understand. How could he even think I was sleeping with someone else?" Lovey cried on the other end of the phone as she told me about Trey's public offense.

"Damn girl. I don't know what got into him. I heard that he got suspended for fighting too. Something must have happened. Did he say who he thought you were sleeping with?"

"Antonio, of all people. I don't even like Antonio like that."

"Antonio? My Antonio?"

"Yeah!"

"Well did you sleep with him?"

"No! Damn, why does everyone think I'm sleeping around?"

"I don't know, but I'll get to the bottom of it."

The next day at school I asked around and was led to Derrick, a witness to Trey's fight.

"What happened with Trey?" I asked.

"What you mean?" he responded.

"The fight yesterday. What happened?"

"Oh, that shit was off the hook!" he boasted. "Antonio told Trey he was sleeping with Lovey and Trey went all Mike Tyson on his ass. Beat him down!"

"Why would Trey even believe some shit like that? Antonio's always joking around. He probably talks about me too," I bluffed, knowing damn well I'd slept with Antonio many times. But I didn't want Derrick all in my business.

"Antonio had proof," Derrick answered.

"Proof? What proof?"

Derrick inched in closer to me and whispered, "Antonio knew that Lovey squirts when she cums."

My eyes widened at the realization of what happened. Antonio only knew that Lovey squirted because I told him. A few days after our trip to the museum, I had called Antonio and invited him over. Of course, he came running, he always did. I asked him to make me squirt. He laughed and claimed that girls don't squirt in real life. He said that was just a movie trick they did in porn to make it seem more exciting.

"Lovey squirts!" I bragged to him.

Then he became obsessed with doing the same for me. He tried. We had sex four times that night. We tried different positions, different rhythms, and different speeds. It didn't work. I didn't even have an orgasm. I completely forgot about the incident. Antonio tried to get with me a few times after that, but I brushed him off. I didn't want him anymore. I moved on to greater things and I was planning to be monogamous and faithful to Jerome.

Jerome was a little nerdy, but he was sweet and smart. We were both interested in history and politics. He wanted to be a lawyer. I still wasn't sure what I wanted to do with my life, but he expressed to me that he thought I'd make a good lawyer too. He was the first person that actually believed I had a bright future and I loved that about him. It was the most meaningful interaction I'd had with any male. I was falling for him and I wanted to make things official. But he had some walls up. We hadn't slept together or made the relationship official though I was determined to do so.

I knew I had to talk to Trey and clear up the misunderstanding. As soon as school let out I high tailed it straight to Trey's house.

"What you want?" he asked when he answered the door.

"I want you to stop being an idiot. How you get in a fight, get suspended, and lose your girl all in one day?"

"She's not my girl, as everyone keeps reminding me."

"Oh, she's not?" I moved seductively close to him in attempt to call his bluff. I knew he cared for Lovey and would resist any move I made toward him. I hoped it would prove his true feelings for her so that he could get over his angry raid. But he called the bluff.

"No, she's not. Besides, you give better head." He put his arms around my waist and pulled me close.

I pushed him away. "Huh, she gave you head? Man, she doesn't tell me anything."

"I know! She's so secretive. No, not secretive. A liar," Trey raged.

"Lovey didn't lie." I calmly spoke as I sat on his couch and nonchalantly crossed my legs. "The only reason Antonio knew she squirted was because I told him."

"What? You!" He stood in disbelief.

"Yep. So, go on, get off your high horse and apologize to Lovey. Now I've gotta go. I've got a date."

"With Jermaine?"

"Jerome! And yes, with him. He's taking me to Red Lobster."

"Classy," he sarcastically responded.

"Whatever, Jerome is none of your business anyway. Lovey is."

I left Trey alone, feeling stupid for believing anything Antonio said. I went home and started getting beautified for my date. When I heard my front door open then slam shut I rushed downstairs and saw my mom's purse on the couch. Most days she didn't get home until well after six. I walked into the kitchen where she was seated with her back turned towards me and her face planted in folded arms that rested on the table.

"Mom, what you doing home so early?" I asked. She sat up and sniffled, her cheeks red and soaked with tears. "Mom, what's wrong? Did someone die?"

"No. Tony broke up with me," she wailed.

"Oh God, mom seriously. You crying over some dead beat nigg…I mean some dude?"

"I really thought Tony was the one. He was rich, and nice, and smart."

"Mom, when are you going to learn? Most men are worthless. You need to use them for what you want, then move on to the next."

"Oh, Erica. You wouldn't understand. You've never been hurt before."

"Never been hurt? Mom, men have been hurting me since…" I stopped myself. I spent years of my life trying to ignore my first heartbreak. I wasn't going to start reminiscing that day. "Oh, never mind. I'm going out with Lovey tonight. We are going to catch a movie and some dinner," I lied. I was fifteen and my mom still didn't allow me to date, so I always used Lovey as a cover.

"Okay, you girls have fun," she said then went back to sulking.

I ran upstairs and started adorning myself with makeup, perfume, and a bad ass outfit. I called Lovey on my way out the door. "Hey Lovey, cover for me tonight?"

"Sure, what's the story?"

"We are going out to a movie, but really I'm going out with Jerome."

"Fine. You owe me though."

I laughed. If Lovey and I actually kept tabs on how much we covered for each other, she'd owe me a hundred and I'd owe her a thousand.

"Oh, Erica, guess what? Trey called me today."

I wasn't surprised – not after the reality check I just gave him. "Yeah, what did he say?"

"He apologized. Said he got some bad information that he later found out was not true."

"Okay, that sounds like a good start. Did you accept his apology?"

"No."

"Why not? I thought you really liked him."

"I did, but how can I be with a guy who doesn't trust me? He didn't even ask if I was sleeping with Antonio. He just assumed it was true and called me out, in public, at that."

"Yeah, that does kind of suck. But maybe you should give him another chance. He…"

"No thanks. I'm good."

I wasn't going to argue with Lovey any further. I figured if Trey wanted her that bad he wouldn't give up after one rejection. He'd keep apologizing until he wore her down. The other line beeped. I knew it was Jerome, so I hung up with Erica and answered.

"Hey," his handsome voice rang out. "I'm here."

"Okay cool. I'll be out in like ten minutes."

I applied some finishing touches to my do, ran down the stairs, gave my mom a kiss then ran out the door before she had a chance to criticize my makeup or outfit. Then I speed walked three blocks down the street until I saw Jerome parked in his black 1993 Acura Integra. Like a gentleman, he jumped out the car and walked to greet me. He was nothing like the men my mom dated; they would just honk when they pulled up. Jerome was a gentleman.

He hugged me tight and whispered, "Hey beautiful." Then he opened the passenger door and welcomed me in.

He was sexy, dressed in a cream-colored sweater, blue jeans, and tan timberland boots. I complimented him nicely with a red sweater, blue miniskirt, and black ankle boots. My short Halle Berry haircut showed off my gold hooped earrings nicely and my makeup was on point. I smiled and stared while he shifted gears.

"Wow, you know how to drive really well."

"Yeah, my uncle taught me. His son died in a car accident. After, he made it his life mission to teach others how to drive correctly."

"Nice! Can you teach me?" I flirted like I was interested. Truth is, I already knew how to drive a stick. I learned when I was twelve. But when it comes to guys you are trying to snag, you have to stroke their ego. Besides, I figured him *teaching* me how to drive would be a good bonding activity for us.

"Sure! Have you ever driven before?"

"A few times. But it was a long time ago. I don't remember much." I didn't want to remember. I wanted new memories to replace the old. I didn't want to dwell on the past.

The conversation went silent and I worried that the silence would bore Jerome. I made small talk. "So, how about those Redskins? They crushed the Eagles last weekend. You think they'll have a chance at the Superbowl this year?" I didn't watch sports, but I kept up with the statistics enough to hold a decent conversation with men. They ate that shit up.

"I doubt it. That was like what? Their second win of the season? They are going to have to do a lot more if they are even going to make the playoffs."

"Mmm," I nodded like I understood. More silence. "So, when are you going to make me your girl?"

He looked over at me and smiled. "My girl? That's what you want?"

"Yeah."

"If you want to be my girl, you can be."

"Yay!" I leaned over and kissed him. I was successful. I snagged me a good man.

The next few months were joyful yet unsatisfying. Every Saturday I went out with him so he could *teach* me to drive. We kissed a lot. But he never tried to sleep with me. I found it odd. But I didn't press him out of fear he might think I was fast. Thanksgiving, Christmas, and New Years passed. We were together each holiday, but sex never happened. I wondered why. *Does he have a small dick that he's embarrassed about? Does he have a disease? Is he gay?* I inconspicuously hinted at my concerns.

"Hey, you notice how it's not the biggest duck that gets the treat? It's how well they paddle," I said suggestively as we overlooked the Potomac River and fed the ducks. He agreed but did not seem fazed by the seduction.

"You know, there are lots of people our age who have STDs. But couples can still prevent the spread with condoms," I said when we were admiring an HIV themed painting by Keith Haring called *Silence = Death* at an art museum.

"Yes, I know. I volunteered at the free clinic before. I felt bad for the people who just found out they had HIV. I am so thankful I don't have any diseases," he said nonchalantly.

"Me too," I responded. *Well, it's not that. And if he was worried that I might be a carrier, he knows now that I'm not. Maybe I can get some now.* But even after that conversation he still didn't budge.

"Are you gay?" Okay, so that wasn't very inconspicuous. But we were at the mall shopping and he said my Nine West boots were cute so I just had to ask.

"No, what makes you say that?"

"Nothing," I responded at the confirmation that he was indeed, straight. I was confused, but I decided to be patient. He was worth the wait.

February 10th I called Lovey. "I don't understand why he won't have sex with me."

"I think it's sweet. Maybe he's waiting for marriage, or at least love."

"Ha! You're such a hopeless romantic. Men don't care about that. All they really want is sex. And if you are pleasing enough maybe they'll fall in love and marry you. Anyway, what are you doing for Valentine's Day?"

"Nothing. I'll be home alone."

"No hot date?"

"Girl, no."

"What about Trey?"

"Mmm, Trey called a few times, sent some flowers and a card. The card was whack. 'Come on Lovey. You know you miss my tongue. Forgive me and let's pick up where we left off."

"He wrote that? He is so tacky… So, did you forgive him?"

"I forgive him, but we are not picking up where we left off. The way he treated me; I don't want a boyfriend capable of saying such things to me. I'd rather be alone."

"You don't have to be alone. Come with me and Jerome. We are going to see *She's All That*."

"No, I don't want to be a third wheel."

"You won't be the third wheel. It'll be me and you and he'll be the third wheel."

"Fine."

"Pick you up at six."

February 14th, Jerome was punctual as usual. Lovey hopped in the back and I held out my hand coaxing Jerome to give me the keys so I could drive. My driving test was coming up soon and even though I was sure I'd pass with flying colors, I wanted as much practice as I could get.

"Dang Lovey, when did you learn how to drive? And a stick at that?" Lovey asked.

"I learned when I was…" I almost slipped. "Jerome taught me. He's a great teacher." I winked at him and he smiled.

"Wish I knew how to drive. I have my learner's, but my parents are too afraid to take me out."

"Let Jerome teach you!"

"Really? On a stick? I don't know…"

"Yeah, it will be fun. He can give you lessons on Tuesdays when I have cheerleading practice. It will be awesome. Won't it Jerome?"

"Yeah sure."

He didn't sound enthusiastic, so I nudged him and he perked up. "Yeah, Lovey, it would be great!"

"Okay, I guess," Lovey said.

Valentine's Day was great. Lovey and I walked arm and arm chatting and laughing while Jerome held our coats and followed. The movie was hilarious and romantic. Then we grabbed a bite to eat in the food court and became deeply involved in a conversation comparing modern art to that of the Renaissance period. Lovey loved art, I loved history, and Jerome found it all interesting. It was probably the best Valentine's Day I ever had. I made sure to drop Lovey off first. Then I stayed in the car a few blocks away from my house hoping instead of letting me go home, he'd take me back to his place. He didn't. He kissed me on the check and said goodnight.

I left the car angry, though I tried to hide it with a smile and a wave.

My sixteenth birthday Jerome had to work, so instead of spending it with him, I went out to dinner with Lovey and my mom. But he made up for it two days later. We had a great time shopping at the mall. He told me he already bought me a gift and was waiting for the perfect time to give it to me. Nevertheless, I coaxed him into buying me two cute dresses and a pair of shoes.

I didn't want the date to end so I volunteered to drive home. But instead, I took a detour, parking in the empty lot of my high school.

"You just turned sixteen and you drive like a pro. Do you have plans to get your license soon?"

"Yep, my mom is taking me to the DMV on Thursday. But stop trying to change the subject. What did you get me for my birthday?"

"You know I started teaching Lovey a few weeks ago. She has been tearing up my clutch. She's not a natural like you."

"Jerome!"

He smiled. "Alright, alright. Here."

He pulled a little jewelry box out of his coat pocket and handed it to me. I excitedly opened it to find a pair of fresh saltwater pearl earrings.

"Oh, I love them," I said as I took off my gold studs and replaced them with the pearls. "How do I look?"

"Gorgeous," he said, then gave me a sweet peck on the lips.

I hungered for more. I leaned over and kissed him passionately then climbed over the stick shift and straddled him.

"What are you doing?" he asked with a big smile plastered across his face.

"I'm getting my real birthday gift."

I started grinding on his waist and I could feel his manhood grow. He was thick and rock hard. I grabbed a condom from my purse.

"Wait, wait," he said. "I shouldn't…"

"Shhhh…" I put my finger to his lips.

He obeyed. I unbuttoned and unzipped his jeans and slipped the condom on his erection. I pulled my lace panties to the side and directed him inside me. I could tell he was enjoying me from the groans that escaped his mouth. I rode him like a jockey. His thickness filled every part of my wet pussy. He lifted up my shirt and started sucking on my nipples which drove me wild. I leaned back and my eyes rolled up with a pleasure that resonated throughout my entire body. He grabbed my ass and kissed me aggressively on my lips, neck, and breast. I could feel the urge build up inside of me until the walls of my vagina started to vibrate uncontrollably. Sweet juices poured from me and saturated his groin. No man had ever made me feel like that.

I was so relaxed after the orgasm I had trouble focusing on riding him. He opened the car door and laid me on the hood where he proceeded to stroke hard, fast, and aggressive, just the way I liked. I could feel the urge rise in me again. As my body seized for a second time, his body did the same. He tensed, growled, and released everything he had built up.

His quickened breathing started to slow as he came down from the orgasmic high. He looked around, discomforted, realizing that we were out in an open in a public area. But it was dark, and no one was around to witness the intense moment we shared.

"I uh, gotta go," he said as he quickly removed the condom.

He held it like it was nuclear waste, looking around the parking lot in disgust until he spotted a trash can a few yards away. He shuffled there quickly, holding up his still unbuttoned pants, and discarded it. He zipped and buttoned up, then hopped in the driver's seat.

"Umm, can you make it safely from here or should I drive you?"

"No, I can make it safe. I'm good."
What happened? Did he not enjoy it?

The next day I caught the metro to Silver Spring and walked three miles to make a surprise visit to his apartment. If he was involved with another girl, the surprise visit would catch him in the act. If not, maybe I would get a second chance at pleasing him better.

I knocked on his door. He answered wearing basketball shorts and a white t-shirt.

"What are you doing here?" he asked.

"I missed you," I innocently responded.

He moved aside to let me enter. So, I knew it wasn't a girl he was hiding. I noticed the paused Tetris game he had up on his Nintendo 64. He went to the controller, unpaused it, and started playing again. I sat on his couch and sighed, emphasizing how bored I was.

"You want to play?"

"No, I want to do something else." I crawled to where he was sitting on the floor and started to massage his ear with my tongue.

"Hey, stop."

He brushed me away and continued to play. When he lost, I leaned over and started to kiss his neck. He winced a little then gave in to the pleasure of it. I pushed him down and laid on top of him, kissing him seductively as he grabbed my ass. I bent down and attempted to pull his pants down so I could start sucking on his member.

"Hey, stop," he said and tried to grab my hand to avoid being disrobed. But it was too late, I could already see what he was trying to cover up. His penis was beet red and covered in welts. I pulled back and looked at him like he was diseased.

"What's that?" I asked. He covered himself in embarrassment and stood up. "You told me you were clean. You lied?"

"I am clean. That is an allergic reaction not an STD. I get it whenever I use condoms. I'm allergic to latex."

"Oh! So that's why you didn't want to have sex with me? Because you're allergic to condoms? You know if you had just told me we could have used something latex free."

"No. it wasn't that. It's just…"

"What? Is it my age? You are only three years older. Plus, the age of consent is sixteen in both DC and Virginia. You won't catch any charges." I inched in to kiss him again, but he stopped me.

"No, it's not that either."

"Then what…what is it?" I was growing more impatient with the charade. No man ever held off on me this long. And for the life of me I couldn't figure out why.

"We're not married!"

"So? What does that have to do with anything?"

"I really wanted to wait for marriage. I tried the whole playboy thing but it wasn't for me. I got into church, got saved, and realized I wanted more."

"You're gay," I stated. I couldn't believe otherwise. No guy saved himself or waited for marriage. My mom dated mostly churchgoers and they were all willing to disrobe on the first date.

"I'm not gay. I am a follower of Jesus Christ and I am waiting for marriage. Or at least trying to. You're not my wife. I'm not even in love with you."

With every word he spoke, my heart was crushed more and more. I couldn't lose Jerome. He was the best man I had ever been with. He read the disappointment on my face and tried to ease the blow.

"I mean, you're beautiful. You're funny. We have tons of fun together. But you're an atheist. How's that going to work?"

"I'm not an atheist. I believe in God," I said attempting to draw closer to him.

"Really?"

"Yeah, sure. Jesus, saving us. Raising people from the dead. You know, The Ten Commandments and shit. Sure, it's believable." I tried to hide the sarcasm in my tone but it spilled out everywhere.

He shook his head, knowing it was bullshit. "We're not equally yoked. This won't…"

"What are you saying? You're better than me? You're too good for me?"

"No. I'm just different. I have different goals. Maybe we shouldn't…"

I put my hand up in his face to stop him from saying anything else. It sounded like he was trying to break up with me but there was no way I was going to let that happen. Who did he think he was? Most men would kill to bed me. I had guys fighting over me all the time. Jerome was a scrawny history geek. He was lucky to have me. I figured I'd give him time to think about what he'd miss out on if he actually terminated our relationship. If I stopped calling him for a few days maybe he'd come to his senses. I dramatically sucked my teeth, grabbed my purse, and slammed the door when I left.

Chapter 8 - Lovey in April 1999

"Hey, my school is having a dance. The Backyard Band will be there. Want to go?"

Erica knew Backyard was my favorite go-go band. Of course I wanted to go. But I didn't want to be bothered by the rumor-spreading fools that went to her school.

"Is Antonio going to be there?" I asked through clenched teeth.

"Probably. But it doesn't matter. Trey is going to be there too. Maybe you guys can rekindle."

"Maybe. Maybe not." I playfully tooted.

"Lovey! Come on!" Erica begged.

"Oh, alright, I'll go."

"Yay!"

"What about Jerome? Is he going to be there?" I asked. I had heeded Erica's advice and started taking driving lessons from Jerome. Driving was not something I was good at, but he was patient and kind. That comforted me. We talked about Erica occasionally. Jerome cared about her. He didn't want to hurt her. But he didn't see a future with her. Erica, on the other hand, knew Jerome was her future husband and I wanted with all my heart for Erica to be happy, so I'd usually put in a good word about her. Maybe Jerome would see past her spirituality and really give her a fair shot.

"Jerome," Erica sighed, "I have no idea. I'm still kind of mad at him. We are still together and all, but I don't know. Maybe I should move on. This dance may be my chance to find someone new. Shoot, you know the best way to get over an old man is to get up under a new one."

"Oh, you so nasty," I teased.

"You know it."

I hoped she would find someone else - a good man that was as into her as she was him. Jerome didn't seem to be coming around and maybe it would be best that Erica moved on.

The day of the dance, I was dressed super cute. I wanted Trey to know what he was missing. I straightened my hair and pinned it up neatly into a high ponytail. I had my favorite skin-tight Guess jeans hugging my hips. I wore black wedged boots and a black wrap shirt that stopped above my belly button. My makeup, curtesy of Erica, was on point. And I was sprinkled in Victoria Secret's Love Spell. When Erica and I walked in, people gawked at our fineness. Boys tripped over each other to make their way over to us and ask for a dance which we happily obliged.

I was dancing with a tall tan drink of water when Trey made his way over to me and interrupted my flow. He took my hand and led me away from the guy I was dancing with. He wrapped his hands around my waist and started slow grinding me.

"You look nice," he said.

"Thanks. So do you."

I danced with several guys throughout the night. But I repeatedly ended up arm and arm with Trey. We danced, flirted, and talked. It felt like old times again. But my guard was still up.

Erica pulled me aside, "You and Trey getting back together?"

"No, why?"

She shrugged, "I think you guys make a cute couple."

I beamed as her suggestion resonated in my ear. I looked at Trey who was standing near the door. He looked towards us, smiled, and nodded. I smiled back and gave a flirty wave. *Maybe I was being too hard on him. Maybe I should give him another chance.*

I planned to sneak out that night, make my way to his house, and surprise him with an intimate reconciliation. I'd wear my sexiest panties and bring condoms just in case things heated up to a point where I could finally lose my virginity. It would be romantic and sexy. I tried to make my way through the crowd so I could whisper suggestive hints regarding my plan. On my way over, Eva and Shantel, some old friends from elementary school, caught my attention. I waved them down and we hugged, talked, laughed, and danced. I was so distracted by the fun I was having catching up with them, I lost track of Trey.

Unfortunately, Antonio was at the dance too. He stared at me most of the night with a lustful smirk on his face. I hoped he would keep his distance, but towards the end of the night he got bold and approached me.

"Hey Lovey, how are you?" he draped his arm over my shoulders.

"I'm fine." I grimaced in disgust as I picked his arm up with two fingers and removed it. His boys were attentively watching us from across the room.

"So, what about me, you maybe hang out later tonight," he suggested as he stroked my cheek.

I brushed him away, "Antonio, hell would have to freeze over before I ever hang out with you."

"Aww, why you gotta be like that?" he slid his hand down my arm and tried to hold my hand, but I pulled away.

"I don't like people who lie about me. Your narcissistic fabrication ruined any chance of me ever wanting to hang out with you. Actually, I don't even want to talk to you now. Your presence depresses me. So, get your tacky ass outa my face."

He started to walk away and then yelled, "Don't no one want your pale stuck-up ass anyway!"

All the guys he was trying to impress exploded into laughter. I wasn't sure if they were laughing at me or him. I didn't care. I rolled my eyes and let the vulgarity roll off my back. The dance concluded without me having to hear any more from Antonio Hightower.

I didn't hear any more from Erica either. Eva and Shantel confirmed what I suspected; she was in a secluded area making out with her new man. I figured I'd catch up to her later. I wished her well and continued to party. At the end of the dance when I walked out into the parking lot I saw a group of people huddled near Trey's car laughing and joking. Erica, of course, was in the center of the action and when she saw me, she waved me over. I had other plans, thus I let her know I was ready to go. Erica was having too much fun, so she was reluctant. But when she saw my desperation, she obliged. We walked home in silence. I went to my house and she went to hers.

I ran upstairs and let my parents, who were already settled in their bedroom, know that I made it home safely. Then I took a long hot shower and adorned myself further in makeup and splashes of perfume. I picked out a sexy satin bra and panties set. Then got dressed in jeans and a hoodie. I snuck out of the basement door and made my way to Trey's place.

Trey usually slept in the basement. I knew if I tapped on his basement window he'd hear me and open the door. I crouched down and looked around the room for him prior to tapping. Then I saw it. He was sitting on the floor against the wall. His head was tilted back and he was moaning. Erica's head was between his legs, bobbing up and down. I couldn't believe what I was seeing, so I inched a little closer. Trey grabbed the back of her head, further directing her mouth as it swallowed his penis.

My heart dropped to my stomach and I felt nauseated. I couldn't believe Erica would do something so conniving after she just told me she thought we were a cute couple. I pulled my hood over my head and quickly marched away. I tried to brush it off, pretending I didn't care. I tried to tell myself he wasn't my man anyway. But in all truthfulness, I was devastated. I snuck back into my house, ran to my room, and drenched my pillow with tears.

Erica called the next day like nothing happened, "Hey girl!"

"Hey," I pretended back. I decided not to tell her I knew. I didn't want to compromise our friendship. Trey, I could live without. But Erica, I needed her. I would have to suffer in silence and get over it. I would have to forgive her without getting an apology from her.

We talked and laughed about situations from the dance - who was fine, who was not, who left with whom, and how Antonio was rejected when he tried to approach me. For a moment, I forgot about the betrayal.

Then Trey called. My mom answered before I could stop her and I mouthed to her, "I'm not here." She covered for me but came to my room questioning my actions later.

"Lovey, what was that all about? I thought you and Trey were friends."

"Not anymore."

"Mmm, you guys use to be thick as thieves back in the day. I miss those days."

"Me too. But you know, Trey has changed. He is more interested in a sexual relationship than a friendship and I am much too young to be thinking about boys right now. I need to be focused on my work. So, I had to shut him down. Right mom?"

That response silenced her quickly and she left it alone.

Monday after school I heard Trey yelling behind me. "Hey Squirt!"

"Oh, don't call me that!" I said and turned around to face him.

"Okay," he said, looking confused and innocent. "So, what's up? I tried to call you last night. Your mom said you weren't in. Where were you?"

"You don't need to know where I've been, who I was out with or nothing. I am not your problem anymore. Matter of fact, don't call me, don't talk to me, don't walk with me. I want nothing to do with you ever again."

I turned to walk away before he could respond.

"What? Lovey! Seriously!"

I heard him calling out again as I walked away, but I didn't look back. I flipped him the bird and never missed a step.

During Tuesday's driving lesson with Jerome I was completely distracted. He decided to confront my lack of attention when the car stalled for a fourth time.

"Yo, Lovey. What's up. You were getting the hang of it. Now you're stalling and messing up my clutch. You okay?"

"Yeah, I'm fine. Sorry. I just have a lot on my mind."

"You want to talk about it?"

I so desperately wanted to talk about it, but I couldn't bring myself to say the words, especially to him. He was technically being cheated on. "No, sorry. I'll do better."

"Okay," he responded. "But if you ever need to talk. I'm here."

We drove a few more miles then came to a stop when I pulled over on the side of the road. "Hey, have you ever been hurt. You know like, by a friend?"

"Of course. I've been hurt by friends, family, girlfriends. It seems like the people you love the most are the ones that hurt you the worst."

"So, what did you do?"

"I prayed."

"Prayed? Like to God?"

"Yeah. It works too. Seems like whenever I pray, the pain eases. Then, after a while, you learn to forgive, forget, and move on. Look, none of us are perfect. We all make mistakes. And when we make mistakes, we hurt others…or ourselves. We hurt Jesus too. But Jesus forgives us. We should forgive others who have hurt us too."

"Well, can you pray with me?"

"Sure."

He grabbed my hands and bowed his head. I followed his lead and waited. There was silence. *Are we praying?* I looked up and his eyes were still closed.

"So do you want to start or should I?" he asked.

"Umm, I don't know how to pray. I've never done it before."

He opened one eye to see if I was being serious. I was.

"Okay, I'll start. Heavenly Father, we come to you today with humble hearts. We pray for the healing of Lovey's broken heart. We pray that you give her the divine gift of mercy, grace, and forgiveness. We pray that you touch and heal every part of her that hurts. We pray that you make her whole and help her get past the obstacles she is currently facing. In Jesus' mighty name we pray. Amen."

As he spoke, I did start to feel better. I thought it was over and I motioned to escape his grip, but he didn't let my hands go.

"Now you try it."

"Okay," I said, but I was nervous and didn't know what I should say or do.

"Just say what's on your heart. A prayer is just you speaking to God."

"Okay…Um God. I've never done this before. In fact, my parents don't even believe you exist. I uh…I'm not sure if you exist either. But I hope you do because I need you. Please help me to get over the pain I feel. Um in God…no, um in Jesus' name I am praying for this to happen. Amen."

"Good," Jerome smiled. "That was a good prayer. Are you feeling any better?"

"Uh, a little."

"Good. You know healing takes time. But you keep praying, you'll get there. And God will show you He is real." He patted my hand. "Now, shall we drive?"

I nodded and took off without stalling.

Thursday night Jerome invited me to Bible study with him. I agreed to go. I wanted to know what this whole Jesus and prayer thing was all about. I knew my parents would degrade my desire to learn more about Christ if I told them. So, I lied.

"Um, I've got a group project at school and we decided to meet at Rebecca's house every Thursday night to work on it."

"Wow sounds like some kind of project," my mom said.

"Oh, it is. It's worth half of our grade." I tried to hurry out of the door before she could question me more, but she caught me.

"So, what's this project about?"

"Umm, Greek mythology. Um yeah. We have to write and direct a play using major Greek gods and goddesses and showcase their various attributes."

"Oh okay…What kind of class teaches that?"

"Um world lit history. Yeah. Literary history of the world. It's a special AP class. Okay, well anyway mom. I gotta go. I'm going to be late. Love you!" I kissed her on the cheek and left. *Literary history of the world? What was I thinking?*

I met Jerome at our usual spot – three blocks up from the house. And we headed to church. The people were so nice and friendly. I got hugs from everyone I met. I felt welcomed, but the affection was overwhelming. We prayed and sang songs, and even though I didn't know the words, I stood and swayed as others sang. The entire encounter felt awkward, but I was comforted when Jerome smiled at me. Then the pastor came out and started to teach from the first chapter of Jonah.

"Oh, I know this story," I proudly whispered to Jerome who nodded and patted my hand while he listened intently. I remembered the story of Jonah and the whale from going to church with Erica and her mom. It was a cute story. But Jerome's pastor broke it down in a way I had not previously fathomed.

He read scripture that depicted the story of a man named Jonah who was called by God to preach to the people of Nineveh. Instead, Jonah went in the opposite direction and caught a boat to Tarshish trying to escape God and his calling. God created a great storm while they were at sea. The crew worried they would perish, and they prayed to their gods for salvation. They cast lots attempting to discover who was to blame for the storm. Jonah confessed that he was running away from God and it was his God that created the turmoil. The crew threw Jonah off the ship and the storms cleared.

"Now, is there a Jonah in your life that you need to throw off your ship?" the pastor asked, piquing my interest with the question. "Is there someone close to you who is not obeying God? A friend, a family member, a significant other who has strayed from their path and is now trying to corrupt yours? If so, you need to throw them off your boat. You need to stop answering when they call you for a booty call in the middle of the night. You need to stop accepting when they pass you a joint, a pipe, a needle, or even some liquor. We are all called to follow our own path. The crew was supposed to go to Tarshish. Jonah was supposed to go to Nineveh. If you enable someone who is on the wrong path, it will only lead to turmoil. If you delete that person from your life, your path will be smoother. And guess what? So will theirs. Look. Read. What happened to Jonah after he was thrown off the boat?"

"He got swallowed by a whale!" some people said.

"A fish!" said others.

"He was swallowed by a fish. The Bible says fish. But he wasn't digested in that fish. He was protected, and the fish led him back on the path he was initially destined for. You need to let your Jonahs go. Not just for your sake, but for theirs."

I'm good! I let Trey go. That was my Jonah. But wait. Is Erica my Jonah too? Nope, I'm not throwing her off my boat. I love her too much. Besides, I'm not sure if this church thing is truly legit. I'm not making life decisions based on possible fraud.

"I'm really glad you decided to come with me to Bible study," Jerome said, interrupting my thoughts.

"Me too."

I looked up when he patted my hand. He was smiling warmly at me. I felt a twinkle in my heart and quickly looked away.

"Did you like it?" he asked.

"It was interesting." I smiled but refused to make direct eye contact. He nodded like he understood.

Over the next few weeks Jerome and I met twice a week. Tuesdays for driving lessons and Thursdays for Bible study. Under his nerdy exterior, he was good company. He was funny, witty, and charming. We laughed a lot. I felt like I could be myself around him. He didn't shame me when I asked him questions about God or the Bible. I wasn't sure if God existed but, I was intrigued and wanted to discover more.

We tried to convince Erica to join us, but she refused. She was always busy. Cheerleading, track and field, schoolwork, and partying were taking up her life. She barely had time for either of us. And she had no desire to go to church or discuss the Bible.

Chapter 9 – Jerome

The oldest of four, I was born and raised on the South Side of Chicago. My parents were poor, but they were devout Christians who went to church every Sunday and faithfully paid their tithes each month. In my youth, I hated their dedication. I found their submissiveness to the faith foolish. They put their tokens in a collection plate which paid for the pastor's nice clothes, nice shoes, nice car, and nice house while we wore rags and struggled to keep the lights on.

When my mother was diagnosed with lung cancer after never having smoked a day in her life, I was done with believing. Yet their faith grew. They stood strong together and prayed for healing. They didn't have any money for her cancer treatments, but they prayed for a miracle. And to my surprise, their prayers were answered. The hospital had a new experimental cancer treatment that my mom decided to take a chance on. Six months later she was in remission with no outstanding medical bills. She still had to visit her oncologist twice a year just in case the cancer came back, but each visit there was a good report. My parents attributed all the success to God. I attributed it to modern medicine.

I was determined to get out of that house and make something of myself. While my siblings and peers ran the streets starting trouble, I kept my nose in a book. In school, I had an animated history teacher. She was white, but she genuinely cared about her ninety percent Black students and often told of the stories left out of our American history books. She told of life in Africa before slavery – the kings and queens, the inventions, the advanced architecture and scientific breakthroughs. She taught of the political struggles between England and America and then later between the North and the South that were predicated on slavery and the abolishment of such. She inspired us with countless success stories of Black men and women after liberation. She taught of the many massacres that swept the country and ended those success stories. She enlightened us about the strategic laws passed and still enforced – designed to continue oppression of Black Americans. She brought the stories of our past to life which helped us understand our present.

It was because of her that I wanted to move to Washington, DC, attend Howard University, and become a lawyer. I wanted to not only get myself out of the ghetto, I wanted to change the systemic racism that plagued America.

Unfortunately, my family was content with their unfavorable American circumstances and unsupportive of my dreams. It bothered me. But when I got that acceptance letter to Howard University with a partial scholarship, I was over-joyed. I left for school and never looked back. I immediately found a parttime job at the American History Museum that helped pay for schoolbooks and my little apartment not too far from campus. Freshman year was the best time of my life. I kept my grades up, loved my job, and was still able to party hard. There were so many females on campus I had a different lady in my bed each month. In my eyes, my life was full.

Then one morning I woke up pissing razor blades. I thought I was going to die. There was a nasty smelling discharge leaking from my penis. I could hear my mom saying to me, "You keep on sinning, one day you gonna reap what you sow."

I sat in the free clinic with a feeling of impending doom. The physician heard my story of highly risky behaviors and decided to test me for everything. He took samples from every orifice. My mouth, my anus, and worst of all, he stuck that big Q-tip in my penis, intensifying ten-fold the pain I was already feeling. He gave me antibiotics that empirically treated for gonorrhea and chlamydia. Then he took a sample of blood to test for HIV.

HIV. The letters hit me hard as he spoke about my risk. I became fixated on the HIV diagnosis. *What if I have HIV? I could die.* The next few days were rough. I couldn't sleep as I was constantly thinking about the possibility of contracting such a disease. For the first time in years, I got on my knees and prayed.

"Lord, if you save me from getting HIV, I promise I will go back to church. I promise I will wait for marriage to have sex again. I promise I will be faithful. Please Lord, help me. Amen."

The next day I got my results. HIV negative. *Hallelujah!* I jumped for joy and went back to church, volunteered for every outreach program I found, and tried my hardest to be abstinent. But that didn't last long. I broke my promise to God with long-legged Keisha after a homecoming party sophomore year. I went straight to the clinic, got tested for everything again, and jumped for joy when everything came back negative.

"Dear God, I am a sinner and I know I need a savior. Please forgive me in your precious son Jesus' name. I don't want to promise that I'll wait for marriage again because…well…my flesh is weak, and I don't want to disappoint you again. But I am done being a playboy. I need your help. I know I am not supposed to have sex prior to marriage, but what if I really love them? How 'bout we do this, the next person I have sex with I promise I will marry."

I felt in my heart that God's rules weren't up for bargaining, but I was a young Black male college student at Howard University. Howard! There were fine girls and fucking opportunities everywhere. I tried to be good. And for the most part, I was successful.

I saw Lovey and Erica walking around the museum where I worked taking pictures and my flesh was tempted again. They were both breathtakingly beautiful. I followed them around like a lost puppy until they caught notice. Lovey didn't seem interested, but Erica did, so I went with her.

I knew she wasn't the one from me a few weeks in. We both loved history but that was the only thing we had in common. Our conversations were awkward and forced. But she was gorgeous and had no problems expressing how much she wanted me. I stuck with her hoping sparks would soon fly. They flew alright, but only physically so. When she came onto me on her sixteenth birthday, I could no longer resist. I took all of her that night and regretted it whole heartedly in the morning. I thought of the promise I made to God just months prior and there I was, failing again.

My first instinct was to break up with Erica. Matthew 5:30 states, "And if your right hand causes you to sin, cut it off and throw it away. For it is better that you lose one of your members than that your whole body go into hell." However, when Erica was in my face, I couldn't bring myself to do it.

Plan B, stick with her until I fall in love with her then marry her. I promised God that I would marry the next person I had sex with. It could have still happened with Erica. Then technically, I would still be keeping my promise to God.

I knew it was a long shot, but I figured I'd try. I stayed with Erica and attempted to mold her into a suitable wife. I introduced her to church, she disliked it. I talked to her about the Bible, she wasn't interested. I tried to convince her to stop partying and wear less revealing clothes, she laughed at me. My plan was failing.

I went to plan C, get Erica to breakup with me. Erica loved attention, I figured if I stopped giving her attention, she'd move on and find someone else. She stuck with me though and for the life of me, I couldn't figure out why. She could have any man she wanted, but yet she stuck with me.

Then Erica recommended I help Lovey out with her driving. I really didn't want to. I figured that she volunteered my services so she could spend more time with me. But that wasn't true. Erica didn't even come to our lessons. At first, I wondered why. She wasn't getting attention from me, maybe she was getting it from someone else. But when I confronted her, she adamantly denied it. She told me she was just busy with school and sports. It made sense so I didn't sweat it.

But Lovey…there was something about her. I was drawn to her. She was beautiful too, but there was more to her than her looks. Our conversations were natural and uplifting. She was humble and reserved, the way I wanted my wife to be. And she was genuinely interested in growing spiritually. The first time I took her to church with me she glowed in awe. Her smile during praise and worship lit up my entire world and woke up parts in me I didn't know were sleeping. She touched my heart, and I felt a flutter every time she looked in my eyes. I wondered if she felt it too. I was too afraid to pursue.

May 6th, 1999 was the day of Lovey's driving test. I knew she was going to kill it. She had been doing so well driving with me. We made plans to meet after the test and celebrate. I bought her a congratulatory gift and was waiting for her in our usual meeting spot.

She didn't look happy when she saw me. "Uh oh. What's wrong?" I asked.

"I didn't pass."

"Oh, no. Lovey I'm sorry. What happened?"

"They didn't have a manual for me to test on. I had to use an automatic instead. I kept trying to use my left foot to clutch but instead hit the brake. I was doomed before I even started."

"Oh. I'm so sorry. Maybe you could ask your parents to teach you on their car."

"I did, but they keep saying they don't think I'm ready. They just want me to be a little girl forever. Anyway, I don't feel much like celebrating…" she turned to walk away but halted when she noticed the gift I was holding behind my back. "What's that?"

"It's for you. Just a little gift to say congratulations. But…"

"I failed."

"No, not failed. Just didn't pass yet. Anyway, I think it's even more fitting now, so here you go."

She took the gift bag from me and looked inside – a purple study Bible, her favorite color. She ran her delicate fingers over the imprinted flowers that decorated the front cover.

"Now, you can read it for yourself."

She smiled and looked up at me with her beautiful bright brown eyes. "Oh, it's beautiful. Thank you so much."

She embraced me tightly and kissed me on the lips then pulled back quickly, shocked and remorseful. Her lips felt right against mine even if it was just for a split second.

"Oh, God. I'm so sorry. I didn't mean to…"

I ignored her rant. Instead, I wrapped my arms around her waist, drew her close to me and passionately kissed her. She relaxed in my arms and we both enjoyed the moment. We let our hearts dance in glee as our temperatures increased a few degrees. I was in love with her. I had tried to deny it. She was my girlfriend's best friend. But I knew it was true. My heart longed to be with her. She was the one for me. And the way she kissed me back, I knew the feelings were mutual.

She pulled away abruptly and walked briskly away saying, "Sorry. I can't…I…I gotta go."

"Wait!" I called after her, but she was gone. I jumped into my car and sped toward her house hoping to arrive before she did. I waited a few minutes until she appeared. Still walking briskly and attempting to talk herself down. She ran up her front porch. I jumped out of the car and ran after her. She saw me coming but ignored me and instead fumbled to get her keys into the keyhole of the front door.

"Lovey! Wait!" I desperately begged, "I love you. I'm in love with you. I want to marry you. And have babies with you. And grow old with you. Please…I don't want this to end."

She turned to me slowly. "But…Erica…"

"I don't want Erica. I want you. You are my heart. You are the one. Tell me you don't feel the same."

"I do. It's just…"

"It's just that we are meant to be. You and me. I know it. I feel it. If you feel it too, take my hand. Come with me."

She reluctantly grabbed my outstretched hand and stepped of the porch. I pulled her close to me, caressed the side of her cheek, and kissed her passionately which set my heart and my loins on fire. We ran hand in hand back to my car. Excitement filled both our eyes as I sped up Georgia Avenue towards my apartment. I lifted her like a newlywed and carried her across the threshold. I gently laid her on my bed and we continued to kiss and caress each other. My desire for her was unmatched. *God knows my heart. God knows my heart.* Is all I could say to justify the passion.

She guided my hand up her shirt where I caressed her perky firm breast. She moaned in satisfaction as I gently massaged her nipple. She smiled as she took of my shirt and tossed it across the room. Then she reached down to where my erect penis was awaiting it's victory and began to unbuckle my pants.

"Wait," I whispered grabbing her hand. "Are you sure you want to do this?" I wanted Lovey's first sexual encounter to be special. I didn't want her to regret anything.

"Yes, I want you." She kissed me. "I want to make love to you." She kissed me again. "I want to feel you inside me."

She nibbled on my ear and I thought I was going to explode. I allowed her to undress me and caress my hardened pillar. I disrobed her and kissed her more passionately. I tickled her clitoris with my fingers until I felt her moisture dripping down my hand. Then I used two fingers to enter her warmth. Her intoxicating moans filled the atmosphere.

"Please, don't stop," she whispered.

I took my time entering her. I put the tip in first. She grimaced and adjusted a little. I let the head of my penis caress her entrance until I felt her relax. Then I put a little more in and a little more. Her intoxicating moans escalated as she clawed my back. Her pussy was tight, warm, and wet. I went deeper and deeper until I was all the way in. I stroked her with a sweet slow rhythm hoping that the pain from her hymen rupture would soon be overtaken with the pleasure of an orgasm. I planned to pull out but the pleasure I experienced being one with her was too much to endure. I moaned, grabbed her hair, and yelled her name to the heavens as I unexpectedly ejaculated inside her.

Her love had me higher than the sky. We gave each other slow gentle kisses as my breathing began to slow and my consciousness floated back to Earth.

"Oh, Lovey. I am so sorry. I didn't mean to…"

She interrupted me with a kiss. "That was beautiful," she said, and we continued a loving embrace until my member recovered.

"Round two?" I asked, worried she'd be sore from the first encounter. But she smiled and nodded her head. Every passion I had suppressed, I released on her. I made love to her until her leg twitched and her walls began to pulsate.

"Oh God!" she yelled.

A sense of pride rose in me knowing I had satisfied her hunger. I continued to stroke her strongly until the urge started to regenerate in me. I pumped harder and faster until I let out a soft roar and grabbed her voluptuous ass tighter and released all my glory deep inside her. We both collapsed on the bed and fell asleep in each other's arms. I had never been in love before, but I knew it was love.

I woke up to the sound of a bus driving by outside my window. Lovey was snuggled in my arms, sound asleep. The streetlight illuminated my window and shone on her face creating an angelic glow. I kissed her softly. She stirred a little. I kissed her again and she stretched and came to.

"Mmmm," she stretched again, looking fulfilled. Then, realizing t was dark outside she sprung up, "Oh my God! What time is it?"

I looked at my clock by the bed. "It's quarter 'til ten."

"Oh, crap! My parents are going to kill me." She jumped out of bed frantically, searching for her clothes.

"Oh, God. I'm so sorry. I completely forgot," I jumped up to help her find her things.

Panic filled her eyes as she mumbled and cried, "Oh my God, my pants. Where are my pants? I can't go home looking like…smelling like… my mom, she's going to kill me. What am I going to do?"

"Calm down," I said as I held her arms. "It will be okay. Why don't you take a shower first then get dressed? You are late anyway. There's nothing you can do about that. What's a few minutes in the shower going to add?"

She adhered to my advice, took a deep breath and said, "Okay."

I lead her to the bathroom, handed her a towel and wash cloth from my linen closet, and turned the water on for her. She stepped in and I stepped behind her, putting soap on her rag and washing her back as she let the warm water fall on her. Her tension lessoned as I massaged the soap suds across her skin. I kissed her on the neck and she leaned towards me – feeling comforted and yearning for more. I kissed her again and held her close to me.

"What am I going to do?" she asked.

"Just tell them your bus came late."

"No, what am I going to do about Erica? I betrayed her."

I released Lovey from my grasp. I wasn't sure what to say. We had both betrayed Erica. I turned Lovey around to face me.

"Look, don't worry about it. I'll handle Erica."

Lovey looked up to the sky trying to hold back tears. Then she sighed, jumped out of the shower, quickly toweled off, and walked out of the door. I followed behind her.

"We can't do this anymore," she said as she quickly put on her clothes.

"What do you mean we can't do this anymore?"

She didn't answer. She left. I hurried to get my clothes on and went after her. I ran down the steps of my apartment, searched the lobby, then went out the door and ran around the block to see if I could catch her. She was nowhere in sight. I hopped in my car and drove to the bus stop, the metro, then to her house. I couldn't find her. I went back to my apartment worried. *What happened? Did I move to fast? Will I lose her forever? Why did I allow my flesh to tempt me yet again? What can I do to fix it?*

All night I prayed and pondered as I inhaled the savory aroma she left on my bed. The next afternoon I went to Lovey's house with a bouquet of daisies. To my surprise, her dad answered the door. He usually did not get off work until much later, but there he was. He was a big brawly man – looking nothing like Lovey. Medium brown skin and eyes to match. He had a few inches on me – height and arm circumference. He folded his strong arms and furrowed his intense brow at the sight of me. His stance was intimidating, but my desire for Lovey overrode my fear.

"What do you want?" he asked in a deep baritone voice.

I stood up straight, poked out my chest and said, "I'm in love with your daughter. Can I speak with her please?"

His stare intensified as he examined me for authenticity. When I didn't back down, he yelled, "Lovey! Someone's here to see you."

"Tell them to go away!" I heard her shout back.

"She don't want to see you," her dad said to me.

I tried to look over his shoulder to see if I could get a glimpse of the beauty that was breaking my heart, but he squared off further.

"Oh, okay. Well can you give her these?"

I handed him the flowers and he took them without saying anything back. I walked away slowly, glancing back over my shoulder to see if Lovey would change her mind, run after me, and hold me in her arms. But she didn't. I could physically feel my heart break into a thousand pieces. It troubled me so much that I became nauseated and weak. My head ached worse than any hangover I had ever suffered. I was defeated. Losing my first true love so quickly was traumatic.

Chapter 10 – Lovey in May 1999

The loss of my virginity was intense and passionate in the moment but afterwards all I could feel was an overwhelming sense of guilt. I had betrayed my best friend, my parents, and myself. When I left Jerome's apartment that night all I could think was run and hide. I ran to the farthest stairwell from his front door and sat there for a few minutes hoping my sobs would not give away my location. When I figured the coast was clear I took the back door out of his apartment building and ran to the metro station. I used the payphone to call home. As the phone rang I prayed my dad would pick up. The last thing I needed was the scolding voice of my angry mother.

Prayers answered, it was my dad who said, "Hello."

"Dad, I need you. Can you come pick me up at Silver Spring Metro Station?"

"I'm on my way!"

I sat there trying to hold back tears when I noticed Jerome's car searching the premises. I crouched down behind a bench, wishing to not be discovered. I stayed there until I saw the headlights from my dad's Tahoe pull into the lot. I ran towards the car and jumped in. I couldn't look at my dad. I knew I'd feel more guilty. Instead, I stared out the window, struggling to prevent more tears from escaping my eyes. My dad didn't say anything and neither did I.

When I got home my mom was on the porch in her robe and slippers. Her ivory face turned beet red and she said, "Young lady, where have you…"

My dad waved his hand, stopping her in mid-sentence. I had never seen him take authority like that and even more surprising was that she obeyed. But I was too distraught to take notice of that rare occurrence and instead, I ran up to my room and cried into my pillow.

At six the next morning, ten minutes before my alarm was set to go off, my mom came into my room, turned on the lights and fussed, "It's time for school miss missy!"

"I'm sick," I responded, and pulled the covers over my head.

She yanked the covers off. "I don't care if you're sick, you get your ass up and off to school."

I pulled the covers back over me. "I'm not going!"

She started to yell and fuss. "You are going to school young lady! You know why? Because I have to work, and I can't stay home with your disobedient ass. And I'll be damned if you stay home by yourself because it is obvious that you are irresponsible and troubled since you want to stay out all night doing who knows what with who knows who…"

"Hold up now honey," my dad intervened, "I'll stay home with her."

"But…"

"I'll stay home with her. You go on and get to work. I have plenty of sick leave. I'll stay."

"Alright fine! But Lovey, you better get up and clean this house. I'll be damned if you stay in bed all day while I'm working."

Dad let me sleep in until ten. Then he came up to my room with a tray of cereal and tea.

"You want to talk about it?" he asked.

"No, not really."

"Is it your grades?"

"No."

"The girls at school?"

"No."

"Are you pregnant?"

I smiled and shook my head no.

"Okay. Well, now that we got the easy stuff out of the way, talk to me. What is it?"

"I…um…had to let go of a friend…that I should not have…that was no good for me," I tried to tell without telling.

"I see," he spoke understandingly. "Well tell me, did this friend hurt you in some way?"

"No…I…I hurt him. But not really. I hurt someone else by being that persons, uh, friend and so I can't be their friend anymore. Because I don't want to hurt that person." I knew I wasn't making any sense, but my dad seemed to follow.

"Uh, huh. Okay, so you can't be friends with one person, I'm guessing it's a guy, because it will hurt another friend, which I'm guessing is a girl?"

I looked to the ground ashamed. "Yeah. Something like that."

"Well, this guy friend. Is he a good friend?"

"Well, yeah!" I smiled as I said it, remembering all that we had done together – church, driving, laughing, talking. I recollected the support he gave when I felt down after witnessing Erica and Trey's entanglement.

"And this girl friend. Is she a good friend?"

"Well, yeah," I said with less confidence, knowing that she had betrayed me, but also remembering the good times we had over the years.

"Well, if this girl is a good friend, then I think she would understand that you want to be friends with this guy and would be supportive."

"Yeah, I guess so," I responded, but I knew that the complexity of my situation was not that simple. Erica would hate me if she ever found out.

I retreated to sulking in bed again until I heard rumbling from downstairs. I got up to explore and saw my dad struggling to clean the kitchen in an attempt to please the demands my mother set on me. I smiled at him as I grabbed the broom and helped. Cleaning was a chore I loathed, but in doing it, my mind drifted from its troubles until the doorbell rang.

I heard Jerome speaking to my father, but I didn't want to see him. I wasn't ready to face him. When my dad called for me, I resisted. My dad came into the kitchen carrying a beautiful bouquet of daisies. My eyes lit up at the sight of it, but immediately dimmed thinking of the trouble pursuing a relationship with Jerome could stir up.

"And where do you want me to put these?" dad asked.

I looked around the room then grabbed a trashcan and held it up. Dad laughed and instead put them in a vase.

"Well, if you don't want them, I'll give them to your mom to soften her up." He winked, and I agreed.

That night Erica called crying and confused. "Jerome dumped me!"

"What? Oh...that's horrible." My feelings were mixed, and I had no idea what to say as I heard my friend wailing on the other end of the phone.

"I mean...it came out of nowhere. Things were going so well. We were having a great conversation and he just blurted it out, 'I don't want to be with you anymore.' Can you believe that jerk? He didn't even give me an explanation. Just hung up on me. He didn't answer when I called him back. I went to his house and he didn't answer the door. I just don't understand why."

I understood, but I couldn't say anything.

"Lovey, please. You've gotta go over there and talk to him. Tell him I love him. Tell him I'll go to church with him. Tell him whatever it is that is the reason for this. I'll fix it..."

"Erica, I can't tell him that."

"Please Lovey. Please you have to. He'll listen to you. You're like a little sister to him."

"Like a little sister?"

"Yeah, that's what he told me. He said he loves you like you were one of his little sisters."

I was too confused to respond. Was I his sister or his lover? Or his friend? Or nobody. Was I trying to help Erica? Or betray her? I had no idea what to do.

"Please Lovey…Please," Erica continued to beg, and I knew she would continue until she had her way.

"Okay, fine! I'll go talk to him."

"Yay, thank you! That's why I love you so much. You're always looking out for me."

Her words made me feel even crappier. I told Erica I'd go see Jerome the next day, but after school I chickened out and went home instead. She called me.

"So, what happened?"

"I didn't go. I…"

"Lovey, you promised!"

After more groveling on her part I promised I'd go the next day.

After school I got off at Siler Spring Metro Station and walked to his apartment. As I got closer to his door, my heartbeat increased exponentially. I knocked, waited a few seconds. *Welp, he's not there. I tried.* I turned to walk away when I heard the chains unlock and a voice call my name like it was a question.

I turned around and made the mistake of looking directly at Jerome. My heart skipped a beat as our eyes met. My mind flashed to how wonderful he felt inside me, groping me, kissing me. I shook it off.

"Hey Jerome. Can we talk?"

"Yes, absolutely. Please, come in."

I walked in and witnessed the aftermath of a pity party. Clothes, pizza, and empty beer bottles scattered throughout the room. He hurried to pick up what he could.

"Sorry, the place is a mess. I uh, had a few friends over and didn't have time to pick up. Anyway, please sit down. What's up?"

"You broke up with Erica."

"I did."

"Why?"

"Why do you think? I'm in love with you."

He reached out and grabbed me by the waist. His touch warmed my entire being. I brushed off the feeling and scooted away from him.

"But she's in love with you."

He looked at me skeptically.

"Okay, she thinks she's in love with you. And she's my best friend. I can't…"

"Are you in love with me?"

Yes, I was in love with him and addicted to his dick. I wanted him to kiss me again. I wanted to feel him inside me again. I knew it was wrong, but my heart and my body said otherwise. All I wanted was him. But I couldn't tell him that. I turned my head and said, "No."

He saw through my front. He knew he had me hooked like a fish. There was no escape.

"You can't even look at me and say it." He placed his fingers on my chin and lifted my face so my eyes met his. "Are you in love with me?" I didn't speak. I closed my eyes as a tear fell. I felt his soft lips press against mine and passion filled my heart again. "Lovey, are you in love with me?" he asked again, kissing my collar bone – sending shivers to my spine.

"Yes, I'm in love with you."

He smiled and kissed me again as he gently pushed me back so I was lying on his couch.

"Say it again," he demanded as he climbed on top of me, landing kiss after kiss on my lips, neck, and chest. I couldn't resist him.

"I'm in love with you," I whispered.

"Really?"

He toyed with me, moving his hand under my skirt, massaging my pulsating clitoris. He moved my panties to the side and started to finger me. He felt so good.

"Yes! I'm in love with you!" I yelled.

"You want me?"

"Yes, I want you. Please!"

He ripped my panties and his shorts off in one swift motion. He opened my legs, hiking the left one up and over his shoulder and then pushed his way past my introitus and began his rhythmic lashing. Each thrust sent waves of pleasure through my entire body.

"Oh! God!" I shouted as I clawed his back. "Yes! I love you!"

My proclamation turned him on more. He hiked both legs up, positioning them on either side of my ears. Then he thrust harder and deeper, reaching my belly button from the inside and holding it there until my legs shook and my body quivered. The intensity of my orgasm sent him into a frenzy, and he began to pump harder and faster. He pulled out just in time to release his warm lava on my belly.

"Damn, girl," he said as he collapsed back on the couch and caught his breath. "I love you too." He smiled as he gave me a kiss on the cheek and then got a warm washcloth and wiped me down.

"You gonna have to get on some birth control or something cause that pussy is too good for me to keep pulling out like that."

I laughed and playfully hit him with the pillow. He laid behind me and held me in his arms as he placed gentle kisses on my shoulder and hand.

"So, will you be my girl now?"

"Oh, look at the time. I've gotta go."

I sat up and he pulled me back down. "Woah woah woah! Where do you think you're going?"

"I gotta go home," I teased. "Not..before...you answer...my...question," he demanded, kissing me between each word.

"For real, I gotta go."

He used his mouth to blow strawberries on my neck. I laughed. Then he tickled me. I laughed harder.

"Alright alright! I give up! I'm your girl!"

He continued to tickle me. "Huh? What you say?"

"I'm your girl!" I shouted.

"Mmmm, hmmm. Thought so." He kissed me again and released me.

As I stood up, he slapped my bare ass cheek. I wanted so bad to jump on him and ride. But I knew if I had, I'd be explaining to my parents why I was home so late from school. Instead, I stuck my tongue out at him in retaliation. He smiled and laid back with his arms folded behind his head. I tried to look sexy while I got dressed, knowing he was staring. But I almost tripped trying to put my socks on. He smiled, still looking infatuated with my every move.

When fully dressed, I leaned over and gave him a peck on the lips. He pulled me closer, tongue kissed me, and grabbed my butt with a firmness that drove me wild.

"How bout you stay a little longer and I drive you home?"

"Mmm, so tempting, but I'm not sure if she can handle any more of you today," I responded, pointing down to my vagina.

He smiled, "We don't have to have sex. I just want to spend time with you."

I smiled and we started kissing again. We stayed in a loving embrace until I really couldn't spare another minute. He drove me to our meet up spot and dropped me off, blowing me a kiss as he drove off. I walked down the street feeling like I was on cloud nine until I turned the corner and saw Erica waiting for me on my step. I still smelled of sex. *Oh God please don't let her notice.*

"Where you been?" she asked in an accusatory tone.

"I went to talk to Jerome like you asked."

"And?"

"And…I can't change his mind. He doesn't want to be with you anymore."

"Did he say why?"

"No."

"You think he's fucking someone else?" she snapped.

I wanted to say, "*I know he's fucking someone else but why do you care? You're fucking Trey.*" But I did not have the courage to confront her. I lied instead. "I don't know. I didn't ask. But you know what, it's been a long day and I got a lot of homework to do."

"It's Friday. You have all weekend to do your homework."

"Not when I have a seven-page paper due on Monday I don't."

"Fuck your paper. I need you. I'm heartbroken. We need to do something tonight like go to a party or something."

I sighed, "Erica, I can't."

"Yes, you can. No paper ever stopped you before. Matter of fact, you've been acting really different lately. We used to hang out all the time and now…you ain't got time for your girl. What's really up?"

"Nothing. I've just been busy and…"

"Oh, come on. I am facing the worst heartbreak of my life and I need you to come and hang out with me."

"Alright already! How about if you let me work on my paper for a few hours, then I'll come hang at your house tonight."

"Mmm, that works!" she announced with a quick change in her demeanor from argumentative to chipper. She gave me a big hug then skipped away. I rolled my eyes, tormented by the fact that I would have to keep my secret lover hidden from her all night. I was horrible at keeping secrets and even worse at lying.

I hurried into the house, showered, then called Jerome. "Babe, I'm going over to Erica's tonight. I'm not sure how I'm going to keep this secret from her."

"Don't keep it. Tell her."

"It's not that easy."

"Yes, it is. Want me to tell her?"

"No, hell no! It'll be bad if she hears it from me but worse if she hears it from you. She'll kill us both."

He laughed, "I think you give her too much power."

"It's not about power. I just don't want to lose my friend."

"Mmm, she's not too good of a friend if you ask me."

"What is that supposed to mean?" I wondered if he knew that she cheated on him with Trey.

"Oh, nothing. It's just…the way she talks to you. It's like she's trying to make you seem less than."

"Naw, she's just outspoken."

"Okay, if you say so. Just remember, no matter what happens. I love you."

"Love you too."

I arrived at Erica's house already dressed in my pajamas and ready for a long night in. But Erica had other plans. She had her black sequin mini skirt and blue tank top picked out.

"Where's your outfit?" she asked.

"Girl, I thought we were just chilling tonight."

"Girl, no! I need to have some fun tonight. And you need to find you a man."

"*I got one…yours,*" I thought, but then said, "Erica, I am tired. And I don't need no man."

"Yes, you do. Come on. You can borrow one of my outfits."

I followed suit, figuring that a night out would make it easier to maintain my secret than a night in. I picked out a pink crop top and some blue jeans. The top was loose on me, but I made it work.

"How we getting there?"

"How you think? Trey."

"Oh God, you still talk to that looser?"

"You still haven't forgiven him? Come on, you know how boys are. It was an innocent mistake."

I rolled my eyes. I could care less that he believed a lie about me. Fucking my friend – that was unforgivable.

"Well, we're going whether you like it or not. Besides, you owe me."

"Owe you for what?"

"For not helping me get my man back. That shit hurt, too. I really loved him."

Erica was laying the guilt trip on thick. "Okay, fine. I'll go."

"Yay!"

Trey picked us up at eleven. He didn't speak and I was fine with that. I sat silently in the back, disgruntled, and looked out the window while Erica cheerfully bounced around in the front. We headed to The Geisha Palace, a small yet popular bar in Georgetown. I didn't feel like socializing, so I sat at the bar sipping on a sprite while Erica entertained a group of mesmerized men who formed a circle around her. They bought her drinks and cooed at every word. Erica just had it like that. She was beautiful and charismatic. Men were drawn to her. And her perky double Ds peeking out from the top of her lowcut tank added to their infatuation. I didn't mind that she got so much attention, it allowed me to slip into the place I felt most comfortable - the background.

Then she called me out, "Not like my friend over there. She'll probably be a virgin forever. Matter of fact, when she loses her virginity, I'm buying her a bottle of champagne!"

I raised my glass of Sprite to her. "Well, I guess you better break out your wallet then." I didn't mean to say it. It just slipped out.

"Wait! What? You dirty little dog. You didn't even tell me?" She sat down close to me. "Please do share the details. Who? What? And When?"

Oh shit. I was trapped. I didn't know what to say. "Umm," I looked around the room trying to think of a believable lie. I made eye contact with Trey who was well out of earshot from our conversation. Straight faced, he raised his glass to us. I smiled nervously.

"Oh, is that why you and Trey aren't talking anymore?" Erica asked.

I shrugged. "Something like that…But, please don't say anything. Especially not to Trey. I don't want him to be embarrassed. You know?"

"Mmm hmm. Your secret's safe with me."

"And me." A surrounding admirer announced as he raised his glass.

"And me," said another.

"And me," another one chuckled.

"Oh, God," I said as I buried my face realizing that all the men who were googling over Erica heard my *confession*. Erica laughed and went on entertaining them for the remainder of the night.

By the end of the night she acquired five numbers. Trey got three. Me – zero. That was fine with me. All I could think about was Jerome. I missed his kiss, his smell, his embrace, his dick. Flashbacks of making love to him consumed my attention. *Maybe I should tell Erica. She'll understand.*

"Hey Erica," I said after we successfully snuck back into her basement.

"Yeah."

I chickened out, "Um, I think I need some birth control. Where did you get yours from?"

"The clinic."

"What clinic?"

"The one on Fourth Street. They got everything. Birth control. STD testing. Abortions. Whatever. They are full service."

"Yeah. But I can't let my parents find out. They would kill me."

Erica giggled, "That's the best part. You don't need to inform your parents for any of those services. It's expensive without insurance though."

"That's okay. I've saved up all my Christmas and birthday money over the years. I'm good."

"Cool! You can go down tomorrow."

"Can you go with me?"

"Naw, I've got a date."

"Okay, next week?"

"Date."

"Okay, when can you go?"

Erica shrugged, "Just go by yourself. You a big girl now."

"Fine, I'll go by myself," I sulked. But weeks passed and I never went.

Chapter 11 – Lovey in July 1999

"Did you ever go to the clinic?" Erica asked me one day when we were hanging out at her house.

"No, but it's cool." Jerome and I were doing fine without it. I snuck him into my basement most nights and we'd make love, then hold each other until my alarm went off in the wee hours of the morning. After much practice, he became an expert with his pull-out game. Erica had moved on, making me feel less guilty about having him as a lover.

"No, it isn't," Erica responded. "I mean, condoms are good, but every girl needs a backup plan. I'm free today if you want to go. Besides, I need a refill anyway."

"Okay."

We took the metro down to Fourth Street, took a number, and waited to be called. Erica went first. She took about twenty minutes, then came out smiling and waving her new pack to show me how easy it was. It comforted me.

"Number 42," a nurse with a clipboard called. My anxiety returned at the sound of my number being called.

"Yes, that's me." I followed her into a cold generic exam room.

"Have a seat," she said, her standoffish tone matching the environment. I obeyed. "Name?"

"Lovey Nicole Patello."

"Date of Birth?"

"June 3rd, 1982."

"Last menstrual period?"

"Huh?"

"Your last menstrual period. When was the last time you had it?" she spoke loud and slow, assuming I was either dumb or deaf.

"Oh, um…" I thought. I was always irregular, but for the life of me I could not remember the day of my last menses.

"Pee in a cup," she slammed a specimen cup on the table next to me before I had a chance to recollect and answer. "Bathroom's two doors down on the right."

"Um, okay," I said, but didn't move.

She looked up from her clipboard. It was the first time she actually looked at me since entering the room.

"Go now."

"Oh, okay. Um, thanks."

I hurried down the hallway, peed in a cup and returned to the room. She wasn't there so I sat back down and waited. Twenty minutes went by without a word and my discomfort intensified. *Maybe they forgot about me.* I stuck my head out of the room and looked around trying to spot someone who could help. A different nurse with a clipboard rushed by.

"Um, excuse me. I think they forgot about me in here."

"What's your name?" she was a lot more inviting.

"Uh, Lovey Patello."

"Okay, I'll check on that for you."

I went back in the room. Another ten minutes of cold silence and I was done. I got up to leave, but before I could, the mean nurse and a doctor came through the door.

"Lovey Patello?"

"Yes, that's me."

"Congratulations, you're pregnant."

"What? I'm what?"

"Pregnant," he said.

"But…that's…it can't be…I…"

I don't have any symptoms and Jerome is diligent about pulling out. Plus, I'm always irregular – it should be hard for me to get pregnant. At least that was what all my friends said. I couldn't be pregnant. It must be a mistake.

"Well, birth control is not one hundred percent. I am guessing this was not a planned pregnancy?"

"No, of course not."

"Well, we do offer abortion services here if you are interested. But first we have to figure out how far along you are. Nurse Jameson tells me you don't know when your last period was. Is that correct?"

"I've always been irregular, so I never really kept track but…I mean…are you sure? Can we run the test again?"

"We ran it twice. You are definitely pregnant. What we can do is get an ultrasound now. It will let us know how far along you are and it will confirm pregnancy. We can do that today if you are willing to wait a few more minutes."

"Um, sure."

They left and I was left in that room with nothing but my thoughts.

Jerome, what is he going to say? What if he leaves me? He's in school trying to make the most of his life. No way he'll want a baby holding him back. My parents – what are they going to do? What are they going to say? Erica, oh God, she'll for sure figure out it was Jerome. She'll understand, right? No, she'll hate me for life. What am I going to do? What about school? College? My life! My life is over.

They returned with a machine. The doctor slapped some jelly on my belly and started massaging it with a wand. On the screen appeared the image of my fetus moving around. I closed my eyes tight. I didn't want to see him…her…it. Tears escaped my eyes as the sound of a heartbeat filled my ears.

"Wow, you're pretty far along," I heard the doctor say.

I didn't want to hear. I wished my ears had an off button. I held tightly to the side of the examination table wishing it were a comforting hand. But it was still and indifferent.

"Measurements say, oh, about twelve weeks."

Twelve weeks? But I was a virgin then. No, I lost my virginity then. Wait what day was it? What day is it? I grew frustrated trying to figure out the dates. I couldn't take any more. I pushed the wand away from my stomach, got up, grabbed some paper towels, and wiped off the jelly. I heard the doctor say something, but I ignored him and ran out of the clinic – tears streaming down my face.

Erica witnessed my escape and went after me. "Lovey! Lovey! Wait! What's wrong? What happened?"

I ran as fast as I could, hoping she'd never catch me, but she had been a track star since middle school. There was no way I was beating her. I felt her grip on my shoulder as she pulled me to face her.

"Lovey! What's wrong?"

"I'm pregnant!" I shrieked.

"Oh honey. It'll be alright," she held me as I sobbed on her shoulder. "Shh, it's okay. I'm sure Trey will understand."

"It's not Trey!" I blurted out, then covered my mouth when I realized what I said.

"Whose is it?" she asked suspiciously, looking at me. I covered my mouth and shook my head. "Lovey, whose is it?"

I couldn't face her. I couldn't face anyone. So I ran.

At home, I paced around my room trying to figure out what I was going to do. When my mom called out to me, "Lovey, phone!"

"I'm not here!" I yelled back.

"But it's Erica!"

"I'm definitely not here!"

I was going to avoid Erica at all costs. I knew that wasn't going to last long. I'd have to confront her one day soon. I paced harder, trying to come up with the words to say. *I could lie. It was rape. No, I couldn't do that to Jerome. I could just get rid of the baby and tell Erica it was some random dude I met at a party. Or I could come clean. Tell the truth. The truth will set you free, right? Maybe? Probably not. It would just make things worse.*

"Lovey," my mom said. She'd come into my room without me noticing. "You're going to burn a hole in that rug if you keep pacing like that. What has gotten into you?"

"Nothing...I just..." I wanted to lie, but I couldn't. "I just need some time and some space."

"Okay, I'll give you some space. But not much. You've gotta talk to someone or you're going to explode."

I nodded my head in agreement. *I've gotta talk to someone. Who can I talk to? Jerome.*

I put on my tennis shoes and made my way out the door. "Mom, I'm going over Erica's to talk. Be home in a few hours."

I walked past Erica's house and headed straight for Jerome's. He seemed happy to see me when I arrived unannounced.

"Babe! What are you doing here?" he reeled me into his arms and tried to kiss me on the lips, but I turned my head and put my hand up. My defensiveness caught him off guard and he unhanded me.

"We need to talk," I said, not looking at him. I knew if I looked at him I'd lose my cool and start sobbing again.

"Okay, what's wrong?"

I took a deep breath and opened my mouth to speak, but weeping took the place of words. Jerome grew confused and ushered me inside.

"Lovey, what's wrong? Did someone hurt you?"

"No, I'm pregnant!"

He raised his hands and stepped backward like I had leprosy. I knew he was going to deny me, kick me out, and forget about me. I collapsed onto the ground and wept louder.

"You're pregnant? With...my child...?"

I felt so exposed holding myself on his living room floor, listening to his rejection.

"Lovey…that's great!"

"What?" I sniffled. "Did you hear what I said? I'm…"

"Lovey…you're having my baby! I'm going to be a dad! That…that's amazing!" He lifted me off the floor and pulled me close to him. "A baby…my baby." He rubbed my stomach then got down on his knees and kissed him…her…it.

"We're going to get married. And I can finish school while you're at home with the baby. Then you can finish school when the baby goes to school. It will be wonderful…"

"But…" I tried to interject.

I didn't want any of that. *Wait to finish school? Be a stay-at-home mom while he still lives out his dreams? What about homecoming? Oh my God – prom, graduation. I've been waiting for these things my whole life – and they'd be gone? Just like that? He wants me to abandon my hopes, my dreams? No! I want to go to college, become an architect, and have fun traveling the world before becoming someone's mother.*

"You don't have to worry about a thing. I will take care of everything."

He kissed me, but I was still in a state of shock. I didn't return the affection.

"You look pale," he said. "You okay?"

I stared into space – my brain couldn't compute his words.

"Come Lovey. Sit down. You should rest in your condition."

My condition? What kind of crap was that? My condition was I needed to get the hell out of whatever twilight zone I was trapped in and live my life.

"I can't…I gotta go…"

"But Lovey, you should rest…"

"I gotta go…my mom…she thinks I'm at…Erica's…gotta go."

"Okay. I'll take you home. You just…don't worry. Don't stress. We got this."

I nodded my head and he escorted me to the spot he usually drops me off. I walked home slowly – still stunned. I unlocked my front door. Sitting on the couch in the living room, arms folded across their chests and anger etched into their countenance was Erica and my mom. They stood like lionesses waiting to pounce on prey when I came into the room.

"Where were you?" Erica started.

"Erica, I got this. Where were you Lovey?"

"I…I…" I had forgotten to tell Erica to cover for me. I was caught. I couldn't think of a lie to escape the series of questions that followed.

"And who were you with?" my mom asked.

"Yeah, and what were you doing?"

"Erica, I got this! Goodness Lovey, what has gotten into you? I mean, lying to my face? How could you? Why? Where were you?"

"I…I…" I couldn't lie anymore. I knew the truth would set me free. "I…was with Jerome."

I felt relief in speaking honestly. Relief that was quickly replaced with fear as I saw Erica's fury develop.

"Jerome! My Jerome?"

"Who's Jerome?"

"Yeah, and what were you doing with *my* Jerome?"

"Erica!" my mom yelled now, growing tired of the cosigning. "Let me deal with…Matter of fact, Erica, just go home. I'll make sure Lovey calls you later."

"But…" Erica tried to plead.

"But nothing! Just go!"

Erica pointed two fingers to her eyes then pointed to me. "I'm watching you," she mouthed as my mom held the door open for her to leave.

"I don't know what you did today. I don't want to know! But you're grounded young lady. No phone. No TV. No going out. Nothing for the next three weeks. Now up to your room."

I ran to my room and collapsed on my bed. The grief I felt was unmatched.

The next day my mom reneged on her word. She broke into my room without knocking.

"Phone," she said, holding it out to me.

"But…I'm grounded."

"Yes. But it's Erica. Don't you think you owe her an explanation?"

"No."

"Well, you do. Here, maybe she can talk some sense into you."

She? Sense? Mom, if you only knew.

Nevertheless, I took the phone and my mom exited.

"Hello." I spoke in an almost whisper just in case my mom was listening on the other side of the door.

"Why were you with Jerome, Lovey?"

"Erica," I rubbed the bridge of my nose and silently prayed for strength. "I am so sorry. I didn't mean for any of this to…"

"You fucked him?" she angrily interrupted.

"I'm in love with him."

She laughed.

"And he's in love with me. He's the father of my baby."

"He doesn't love you. He just wanted to fuck you and like a dumb ass you let him. He's going to be on the first flight back to Chicago now that you're pregnant."

"Erica it's not like that. I…"

"You're so full of shit. All that *I'm innocent* bull you've been talking. You are the worst kind of friend. The one who pretends to be down for you and all along is stabbing you in the back. I would have never done anything like that to you," she had the audacity to say.

I was done playing nice. She needed to hear about herself.

"Erica don't play games with me. I saw you sucking Trey's dick."

"What! What the fuck are you talking about?"

"After the dance. I saw you. I went to Trey's house that night and saw you in the basement."

"Wha...We...How..." Shocked, she stuttered. "Well...I had Trey first!"

Her statement slammed down like a ton of bricks on my heart, crushing its delicacy. How dare she even try to justify sleeping with Trey when she practically forced him on me. Repeatedly she advised me to forgive him and take him back. Yet all the while she was sleeping with him. Nevertheless, I let that shit go. I stayed her friend despite it. And she couldn't forgive me for Jerome? She was sitting there acting virtuous and judging me when her actions were just as foul. *Oh hell no!* I wasn't having it.

"First! Bitch, you had everyone first!"

Erica gasped. My words piercing her soul. "You know what? That's it. We are done! You are no longer my friend. You are dead to me."

"No, you are dead to me!"

"Fine!"

"Fine!"

"Fine!"

We both hung up on each other and that was it.

I paced more – angry, hurt, fearful.

Shit, look at the mess I've gotten myself into. I messed up a perfectly good friendship. I messed up my perfectly good life. And for what? For love? For sex? Damn. What if Erica is right? What if Jerome really doesn't love me? What if he really does leave? Why the heck did I even sleep with him? I wasn't trying to get revenge. Was I? I didn't care about Erica and Trey. Did I? No. I just wanted to feel love and intimacy. And Jerome – he loves me. And I love him. Right? But…what if…he doesn't?

Chapter 12 - Lovey in August 1999

There was no way I was going to keep the baby. I called the clinic for an appointment the next day.

"So, because you are so far along you need to have a procedure done. The procedure can be a little painful. You have the option of getting sedation. However, you will need to have someone drive you to and from the clinic," the nurse on the other end of the line informed me.

"No thanks. I don't need any sedation. I just want to get it done."

"Okay, well I have you scheduled for Thursday the fifth at one pm. Is that good?"

"Yes, perfect."

"Wonderful. Be sure to arrive fifteen minutes early for paperwork. I will see you then."

"Thanks."

Thursday couldn't come fast enough. I left home that morning in my school uniform and headed to the metro like usual, but instead of taking the red line to school, I took the green line to the clinic.

That cold sterile room was even colder than I remembered. I was given a robe and told to undress. I had never felt more alone than I did sitting on the examination table waiting for the doctor to come in. I thought about the little life inside of me. Was it a boy? A girl? Did it have my eyes or Jerome's? Would it be smart? Could it be the first Black president? I shook off the thoughts. *Prom. College. Travel.* Those were more important to me. Having a baby would have to wait.

"Lovey Patello are you ready?" a male doctor asked as he walked into the room making eye contact with only my chart.

"Yes, I'm ready."

"Nurse Fine will be assisting me today. She can inform you about what is happening if you would like."

"No, can we just hurry up and get this done?"

"Sure."

They pulled out some metal stirrups and asked me to put my feet in them. Then I felt a speculum penetrate me. It was cold. It pinched and I felt pressure and began to cramp. All I could think about in that moment was how could sex feel so good and a speculum so uncomfortable. A dick and a speculum go into the same place, but the sensation is totally different.

"Okay, I'm going to give you some numbing medication. You are going to feel a little prick."

That little prick was more like a dog bite in my vagina.

"Ow, fuck!" I said, clenching hard onto my gown.

The temperature in the room suddenly felt like 100 degrees. Beads of sweat formed under my armpits. Nurse Fine noticed my discomfort and grabbed my hand telling me to squeeze. Who would have thought such a simple touch could bring so much comfort? She flashed me an understanding smile and patted the back of my hand. I relaxed a little.

"Okay, I'm going to dilate your cervix. It may feel a little crampy."

I heard some metal clinking then I felt the worse menstrual cramps of my life. It felt like my insides were being ripped out.

"Okay, now I'm going to apply some suction. You're doing good Lovey. You're doing good."

I heard the sucking and scraping. I felt painful vibrations in my womb. I imagined my baby being torn apart and sucked out into the vacuum hovering between my legs. The pain was excruciating. I squeezed harder, moaned louder, and felt the wetness on my cheeks as tears escaped my eyes. The pain was both physical and emotional. The suctioning only lasted eight minutes but it felt like a lifetime.

Finally, he removed the plastic tube; but my pain did not resolve. "Okay, let's get you cleaned up," he said as he mucked around in my vagina. I felt pulling and tugging and pressure. "Nurse Fine, can you get me some more gauze and another chucks pad?"

"Yes sir," she said and carefully removed her hand from my death grip.

"Is everything okay?" I asked.

"You're just having a little more bleeding than usual. But we are going to try our best to get things under control."

I lifted my head and shoulders a little and looked at what was on the table. Several large Q-tips and gauze pads soaked in blood and tissue – my blood, my baby's tissue. A nauseating wave rushed through my body. "Oh, God," I whispered. The room started to spin and my vision tunneled. I fell back on the table, drenched in sweat.

"Dr. Wright, she doesn't look so good," I heard the nurse say just before I passed out.

When I came to, the first thing I saw was a bright light above my head. I felt pain everywhere – my stomach, my vagina, my legs, my back, and my head. Vomitus rose from my gut and made its way to my mouth. I leaned over quickly and a nurse rushed to my side holding a plastic container.

"There, there," she said and patted my back gently.

All that came out was stomach acid, but it felt like I needed to get out so much more. I dry heaved which made my stomach cramp worse.

"What happened?"

"You had some complications with your procedure. You lost a lot of blood. But the doctor was able to stop the bleeding."

I sat up, which intensified the pounding in my head. "Mmm, what time is it?"

"It's four…"

"Four! Oh crap. I've gotta go."

"Not so fast," she held me down. "It is not safe for you to drive. You need to call someone to take you home. Doctor's orders."

"I'm not driving. I'm taking the metro."

"Even worse. We can't have you walking around during rush hour in your condition. Can you think of anyone who you can call that will pick you up?"

I thought about it. *Dad? No. Mom? No. Erica? Oh, hell no! Jerome? Hmmm…no. I couldn't have him find out about the abortion like this. Trey? I had no other choice.*

"I have someone. Can I use the phone?"

"Sure."

I dialed Trey's number hoping he had made it home from school already.

"Hello?" he answered.

"Trey, I need your help. Can you pick me up from 1120 Fourth Street?"

"If I do, what you going to give me?"

"Trey stop playing. This is an emergency. I really need your help."

"Alright, fine. I'll be there in twenty minutes."

"Thanks."

I felt so weak. I barely had the strength to put the phone back on the hook. I collapsed back onto the gurney and rested until the nurse informed me my ride had arrived. I needed help to walk to the car. I know I looked awful. Trey's face lit up with concern at the sight of me.

"Damn, girl! You look more pale than usual. You've always been light skinned, but now you look like a ghost. I can almost see through you."

I didn't respond. I just slouched down in the passenger's seat and concentrated on not vomiting in his car.

"So, you gonna tell me what happened?"

The look I gave Trey in response shouted, *"I ain't telling you a damn thing."*

"Can you at least tell me whose baby it was?"

I gave him the same look. The rest of the ride home was silent. I made it to my bed ten minutes before my mom arrived. I told her I must have ate something bad at school and she allowed me to stay home the next day. I slept all day Friday. Saturday morning I felt like myself again – physically. Mentally I was riddled with guilt. I was glad I was still on punishment because it made it easy to avoid phone calls from Jerome. He called almost every day. I could hear my mom pick up the phone and say, "No, sorry Jerome. She is still on punishment." Trey called a few times. I didn't want to talk to him either. Erica never called. One part of me hoped she would try to rekindle the friendship or at least check to make sure I was still alive. Another part said, *"Fuck her. She's not your friend anyway."*

Diarrhea kept me up most of Sunday night. I figured it was due to stress, but when my mom came to wake me up Monday morning she noticed my misery and immediately got the thermometer.

"One-o-four," she said reading the thermometer. "Well, you're not going to school today."

"But I have a test," I protested.

I had been stuck in the house feeling sorry for myself for four days and I was eager to get back to my normal life. I hoped schoolwork would distract my mind from my life. The last thing I wanted to do was lay in bed continuing to feel sorry for myself.

Lovingly, my mom responded. "Tisk tisk. My Lovey. You've always been a go-getter. I love that about you. But you are sick, and you need some rest. I'll get you some lemon ginger tea. That should help."

I nodded and obliged. My mom stayed home from work and took care of me. It took a few days but with love, care, and lemon ginger tea, I recovered and was happily back in school on Thursday. I didn't even care that in each class I was overloaded with assignments I had missed and needed to make up. I happily accepted the challenge of having it all completed by Monday.

I was energized on my walk from school to the metro station when I heard, "Lovey!" *Shit!* I plastered on a fake smile and turned around.

"Hey Jerome," a poor attempt to conceal my guilt.

"Babe, I've been trying to call you all week. Are you okay? Is the baby okay?"

"Yes, we are fine…um…actually…no. I'm fine."

"The baby?"

My heart melted as I stared into Jerome's eyes. The look of concern and hope Jerome presented was exactly what I was trying to avoid. He desperately wanted us to be a family. I killed that possibility. If he found out, he'd leave and never forgive me. I couldn't let that happen. I loved him. I needed him. I missed making love to him. I wanted us to share our life together and one day start a family – just after prom, college, and traveling the world. I knew he wouldn't understand my reasoning, so I lied.

"Um, the baby. I…uh…had a miscarriage."

I watched his heart break. "Oh, baby. I am so sorry." He pulled me close to him and kissed my forehead. "It's okay. I guess it just wasn't our time."

Exactly, it wasn't our time. I was happy. I got away with the abortion – Jerome and my parents remaining oblivious. Jerome whisked me away to his apartment and held me until I fell asleep. It felt good, like I had another shot at life and love.

Chapter 13 – Jerome in August 1999

Years of follow up doctor visits with good news and God praises until one day a malignant report surfaced. My mom said the cancer was back and it was worse. It had spread to her lymph nodes and they wanted to start chemotherapy. She was strong despite her news. I was devastated.

"Do you need me to come back to Chicago?"

"No baby, you know God's got this. You finish out school and don't worry about me."

If it were just school, I would have ignored my mom and jumped on the next plane to Chicago to be by her side. But I had school and Lovey to think about. When she told me she was pregnant, I was overjoyed. I had every intention of marrying her and raising this child with her. I even went to the jewelry store to pick out a ring. But apparently those weren't God's plans. News of the miscarriage hurt. But I knew that Lovey needed me, so I was going to be strong for her. I planned to stay in DC long enough for us both to finish school, then we could both move to Chicago to take care of my family and start our own.

Lovey laid comfortably in my arms. I watched her sleep. Her soft breathing was music to my ears. All I wanted to do was protect her and ease any burden she might have felt. I held her tighter when she stirred and kissed her on the forehead. Her eyes blinked open and she smiled as she regained focus. She gave me a soft sweet kiss on the lips.

"Hey," she said.

"Hey," I smiled back.

"I gotta get home."

I agreed and took her back to our usual drop off spot. As she walked down the street towards her house, I starred at her backside and thought, *I am definitely staying.* I drove home, content with my decision until I got to my front door. Erica was standing next to it looking flawless. She wore a short skirt exposing her smooth legs. Her arms and legs were crossed as she leaned up against my door.

"Hey lover," she said.

"Erica. What are you doing here?"

"I came to see you." She flirtatiously stroked my collar. "Can I come in?"

"I don't think that's a good idea. I have a girlfriend."

"She ain't me though."

She pulled me closer, and I was engulfed in whatever sweet perfume she adorned herself with. Resisting her, I pulled back and crossed my own arms.

"It's Lovey. Isn't it?" she asked. I remained stoic. "Lovey only cares about one person and one person only. Herself. You think she's sweet and innocent? She's not. You think she's actually down for you? She's not."

"Well, neither are you."

"What's that supposed to mean?"

"Trey," I called her out.

"Huh," Erica gasped. "That little bitch! She told you I slept with him didn't she?" "Actually, no. But you just did. Now, if you'd excuse me."

Erica, shocked, stared wide-mouthed as I pushed past her to open my door. I always suspected she had something going on with Trey. The way he looked at her and the way he resisted me. There had to be something more to the relationship than what they led on. But out of respect for Lovey, I kept my mouth shut. Erica gave me the confirmation I needed and her seductive attempts to ruin Lovey and I had no merit.

"Well…well…Lovey's not pregnant anymore! Did you know that?"

Erica was really provoking me. The loss of our baby was a sore point and for her to use it as a means to break us up was appalling.

"Unlike you and I, Lovey doesn't keep shit from me. I know she miscarried. She told me herself. Now, if you'd please remove yourself from my presence."

A mischievous grin crept across Erica's face. "She didn't miscarry. She got an abortion."

"Yeah, the fuck right."

"She did. Trey drove her. You don't believe me? Ask him."

I closed the door in her smirking face. *An abortion? No, fuck no. She knows how I feel about abortion. She knows how God feels about it. She goes to church with me all the time. She'd never. Would she? Maybe she had me fooled. Maybe she isn't as innocent as I think. There is no way I'm asking Trey anything. I know what kind of man he is. He would sleep with Erica, Lovey, and anyone else with no regrets if given the opportunity and he'd lie to do it. But maybe I should at least confront Lovey. If anything, she can confirm that Erica is full of it.*

I called Lovey. She answered, chipper as usual. "Hey my love."

"Hey. Am I going to get to see you tonight?"

"What? You didn't get enough of me earlier?"

I snickered, "You know I can never get enough of you."

"Well, I'll see you tonight then. I've got to go do my homework now though. Love you."

"Love you too…oh wait. Lovey, you know you can tell me anything right?"

"Yeah?"

"Well, do you have anything to tell me?"

"Like what?"

"Anything. Like…anything."

"No, everything is good."

I could hear her innocent smile through the phone. It was just like I thought. Erica was a liar and I had nothing to worry about.

"Okay Boo. I'll see you later then."

"Okay. Bye."

It started to pour down rain on my way to Lovey's house that night. But I didn't care. I was feeling good. Plus, I figured the roll of thunder would accentuate our love making ambiance. I parked a block away from her house as usual and walked in the rain unfazed. I skipped joyously as I approached her house, feeling like a good kid on Christmas morning.

Tap. Tap. Like usual, I knocked on her basement window. Our little code for *"I'm here. Open the door if the coast is clear."* I heard the back door open and I saw her beautiful smiling face. I lifted her up in my arms and kissed her all over her face. She giggled.

"I missed you," she whispered.

My heart was flooded with her sweetness as we settled down on her couch. I wrapped her in my arms and held her tight as she continued to watch whatever movie was playing on television. I wasn't interested in the movie. All my attention was focused on her. The smell of her curly hair caused my member to thicken. My breathing grew heavy and coarse with desire. I rubbed my nose on her soft neck then gently placed kisses there. A shallow moan escaped her lips as she wiggled, causing her voluptuous butt to rub against me in just the right way. She knew exactly what she was doing. I started to inch my hand from her stomach to her breast. It had been weeks since I last made love to her and my cravings were immense.

She grabbed my arm. *She never stopped me before.* I kissed her and she wiggled out of my grip. *Maybe it was too soon after the miscarriage or maybe she just started her period.*

"You okay?" I asked, confused about her resistance to my advances.

She crossed her arms as a look of concern hijacked her face and tears filled her eyes.

"I...I..."

"You what?" A mix of emotion invaded my happy space. Anger. Concern. Worry. Fear.

"I have to tell you something."

No man wants to hear that. I sat up, giving her my full attention.

"I…um…didn't miscarry. I..uh…"

I stood up and cut her off. "I don't even want to know," I said walking towards the door. *No, I have to hear it from her.* I stopped and turned to her. "Actually, what do you have to tell me?"

The tears flowed from her eyes. She was hurting, but not half as hurt as I was feeling.

"I aborted it."

The words echoed in my ears and suddenly I felt sick to my stomach. Erica was right. Lovey was the liar. And I was the fool.

"I should have known you were too good to be true," I said as I walked out the door. In the distance I heard her pleading for me but I was too angry to acknowledge. I was done.

Chapter 14 – Lovey in September 1999

Loosing Jerome unleashed a pain I never knew existed. I felt like an Olympic track runner losing a leg. Like an opera singer losing her voice. I couldn't breathe without him. Robotically, I woke and went to school every day then cried myself to sleep every night. Food was bland, colors dull, life was monotone. Every part of me missed him. I tried to call; he didn't answer. I left messages pleading for forgiveness; he didn't respond. It took a couple of weeks, but I mustered up enough courage to go to his apartment and knock on his door. Impatiently I waited, listening for any signs of life behind his front door. But there was none.

"He's gone."

I heard the voice of an older lady from behind me. I turned and saw one of Jerome's neighbors struggling to make it down the hall with bags of groceries in her hands.

"Ma'am, let me help you with that," I offered.

She smiled and handed me a few heavy bags. "Thanks dear."

"Do you know when Jerome's coming back?"

"Far as I know, he's not coming back."

Panic flooded my heart. *What do you mean he's not coming back?*

"He went back to Chicago. Something about his mom being sick? Anyway, he packed up all his stuff, gave his final month's rent, and left."

"But school. He just started his senior year. He has to come back."

The old lady shrugged her shoulders. "Well, we are here," she said landing at her front door. "Thanks for your help. God bless."

My heart sank to the floor and nausea overpowered me. I ran down the stairway but vomited before I could make it outside. I didn't have the strength to go on I curled at the bottom of the steps and cried until my shirt was soaked and my eyes ran dry. I couldn't get up. I didn't have the strength to go on. Jerome may not have loved me enough to forgive me or enough to stay; but I was sorely in love with him. Every inch of me missed him and hurt from grief of that loss. I felt like Jonah. Off-course and alone.

And then, from deep in my spirit a voice spoke, "Get up!"

But I didn't want to. I couldn't. I was empty.

"Get up!" the voice said again. "When Jonah was thrown off the boat he was not alone. I was there. When he sat in the belly of a fish, I was there. Though uncomfortable he was safe and upheld. And if you get up, I'll uphold you too." I wasn't sure where the voice was coming from. Was it God? Was it my subconscious? But I do know that the voice was filled with strength, love, and courage. It impowered me to continue with my life. To not allow this disappointment to keep me down. I wiped my red tear saturated cheeks, inhaled deeply and went home.

The next morning I woke with a burning pain in my feet. I tried to wiggle my toes to see if I could shake the feeling but there was no relief. I attributed the feeling to stress; but when I tried to get out of bed my legs refused to work and I collapsed. My mom, who must have heard the thump, rushed to my side.

"Fell out of bed?" she giggled.

I looked up at her. Fear must have been apparent in my gaze for her joy immediately shifted to concern.

"Lovey, are you okay? What's wrong?"

"My legs. They fell asleep and they won't wake up."

She bent down and tried to help me up but couldn't budge me.

"Try to shake them," she suggested.

I focused my brain on moving my legs, but my muscles didn't even twitch.

"I am trying. It's not working." I tried to suppress the panic I felt rising and I could tell she was doing the same.

"Charles!" she yelled for my dad. "We need your help!"

He came rushing in. "What! What's wrong?"

"My legs! They're not working."

"What do you mean they're not working?"

"She fell out of bed and now her legs don't work," mom chimed in.

My dad leaned back and contemplated the seriousness of the issue. Was I just being a dramatic teenager whose legs fell asleep or was this a true emergency? He bent down and pinched me.

"Ow!" I said, though my legs didn't retract.

"Oh, so you can feel?"

"Yeah. I felt that."

"So, you're not paralyzed. Girl, get up and go to school."

I wiggled and squirmed trying to get off the floor but from my hips down I was flaccid. My parents watched me struggle – their concern growing with each attempt.

"Lovey, stop playing," dad said.

"I'm not, dad!" I yelled in frustration.

My mom looked helpless and unsure of what action to take next. The burning pain intensified and radiated up my legs and to my back. My dad reached down to pick me up. Everywhere he touched was tender.

"Ow, it hurts."

"What hurts?"

"My legs. They hurt and they won't move. What's wrong with me?" I sobbed.

"Let's get her to the hospital."

My dad attempted to pick me up and stand me on my feet but when that failed, he scooped me up in his strong arms and carried me to the car. In silence we rode. I could see my mom quickly try to wipe her falling tears. She was trying to hide her fear from me. My dad just looked serious. He parked in the ER parking lot of Howard University Hospital and carried me inside.

"I need some help here!" he yelled.

My arms were gripped tightly around his neck and I buried my face in his shoulder trying to hide from the pain that steadily intensified.

A nurse came to his rescue. "Sir, what seems to be the problem."

"She can't move. And she's in pain. Please help her."

"Trudy, bring a wheelchair over pronto!" she yelled to a nearby staff.

The young lady dressed in white scrubs hurried to find a wheelchair and they rushed me back to an examination room while my parents held each other and followed.

"What do we have here?" a tall thin doctor with thin round glasses asked as we rolled past.

"Apparently she can't move."

"Take her to bay three. I'll be there in a few minutes."

The nurse did as she was told and started to get my temperature and blood pressure.

"Hmmm, no fever. Did you have some kind of trauma?"

"She fell off the bed," my mom answered before I had a chance to.

"Actually, my legs stopped working before I fell off the bed," I corrected.

"Hmmm, have you been under any stress lately?"

"She just broke up with her boyfriend and…"

"Mom!"

How did she even know that?

"I'm sorry honey. Go ahead."

"Um, yes ma'am. I have been under a lot of stress but…"

"And how old are you?"

"Seventeen," I said, confused to why she was worried about my age and social life when I couldn't move my legs.

Noticing my disdain, she turned to my mom and asked, "Is she a good kid or does she tend to be more of a rebellious teenager?"

My mom looked just as frustrated as I felt. "She's a great kid. But what does that have to do with anything?"

"Well, sometimes teenagers do things like this for attention. Either that or they have been experimenting with…umm…substances."

"I'm not making this up!"

"And my daughter has never done drugs in her life. She's a great student. Honor roll at Georgetown High School every year."

The doctor rushed into the bay interrupting the building tension. "Hi, I'm Dr. Watson. What seems to be the problem?"

"Hi! I'm Dianne and this is Lovey, my daughter. She is a great kid, and she hasn't had any health problems before. But today when she got up to get ready for school she couldn't move her legs."

"Hmmm," he leaned over to examine my legs, lifting one up. I grabbed my father's hand tight as the simple touch inflamed my skin.

"It hurts?" he asked.

"Yes, it burns."

"Hmm, Nurse Stevens please give her one milligram of morphine through an IV."

"Yes sir," the nurse said, then scurried away.

The doctor bent down and moved my leg around, then my foot. He took out his little reflex hammer and tapped my knee. There was no response.

"Hmmm," he said.

"Doc, what is it?" my dad asked.

"I'm not sure, but I think we need to run some tests on her. We are going to admit her for observation. Is that okay?"

My parents both nodded in response and Dr. Watson poked his head out of the curtain and let Nurse Stevens know to prepare me for admission.

"Has she been sick recently?" he asked, sitting back down in a chair next to me.

"Yeah, she had diarrhea a couple of weeks ago, but it only lasted a few days. Other than that, she's been a perfectly healthy kid."

"What about procedures or surgeries? Has she ever had anything like that?"

"No, never," mom said.

Guilt riddled me as I remembered my recent abortion. *Could that be the culprit of my condition? What if Dr. Watson went on believing that I never had any procedures and misdiagnosed me? Maybe I should tell the truth. But my parents. They would be so disappointed in me.* As I contemplated, Dr. Watson continued asking my parents about my medical history and events leading up to today's condition.

"Actually…" I said, interrupting. "I did have a procedure." Shame filled my heart as I looked back and forth to my parents' curious faces. "I, um, had an abortion last month."

"What! You what?"

"I'm so sorry," I whispered to them. I didn't think I had tears left to cry but copiously they poured.

My dad squeezed my hand tighter and my mom wrapped her arm around my shoulder giving me a supportive hug. They didn't say anything, but I felt what they meant. *"We are disappointed, but we still love you and wish you would have come to us before now."*

Dr. Watson gave an understanding nod like he had witnessed similar situations a million times before. Nurse Stevens came back accompanied by another nurse.

"This is Mrs. Lightner. She is one of the pediatric ICU nurses and she'll be helping me give you an IV. Okay?"

I nodded my head as they explained the process of putting a little tube in my arm so they could easily take blood and give me medications. The doctor called off a bunch of words, letters, and numbers.

"Can you get a Chem seven, a CBC, an ESR, HCG…"

The nurses seemed to understand his commands, but they were devoid of meaning to me. All I could feel was guilt and pain. I closed my eyes tightly and squeezed my mother's hand while Nurse Lightner placed the IV, took blood, and injected me with numbing medication. Dr. Watson continued with his questions and his poking and prodding.

"What about your family? Do any medical conditions run in your family?"

My parents looked at each other then back at Dr. Watson. They looked at me with sorrow in their eyes. My dad squeezed my hand tighter.

"Umm," my mom started. "Actually, Lovey is adopted."

"I'm what?" I asked.

"Adopted kiddo," Charles smiled, his nervousness evident.

"Sweetheart, we were going to tell you but…"

"Adopted?" *Adopted? Did I hear that right? There was no way I could be adopted and not know it. Could I?*

"Well, I see this family has been holding a lot of secrets," Dr. Watson said.

We all looked at him feeling shamed.

"How about we let you guys talk while we run those tests. If you need any of us just press this button right here on the wall."

They all left.

"Abortion?" mom asked.

"Screw that. Adoption?" I responded.

"Hey," dad scolded me. I would have fussed more but the medication they injected was starting to take over. I floated like I was half asleep and half awake. It was a strange feeling, but I didn't mind it because my pain was disappearing.

"Honey," mom pulled up the chair to face me and she gently took my hand. She could see the glaze in my eyes and the loopy smile that stuck on my face despite the weight of the situation. It calmed her. "An abortion? When? Why? Who?"

"Mom," I slurred, high off morphine, "I slept with Jerome. Like a lot. But I loved him. And he left. I was so sad."

Charles angrily shook his head and paced. He looked like he was plotting to kill Jerome.

"Dad! He was good. I was bad. He wanted to have a baby with me. I wasn't ready. So, I got rid of it. Me. On my own," I giggled. "I regret it. I think about what my baby would have been like all the time."

Mom seemed to understand. She patted my hand and looked up at her husband. "We, uh…couldn't have kids. We were on a waiting list for adoption for a long time and one day we got a phone call. Baby girl abandoned at hospital." Dianne half-smiled as she looked around the room. "This hospital. Honey, this is where you were born. Your birth mom was…uh…into drugs. She left you here a day after you were born. You were born addicted to cocaine and heroin."

"My mom? She looked…like me. That's why I don't look like you guys? I thought I got my nose and hair from grandma."

The person I formerly knew as my only mom smiled, "Your mom was White."

"White! I'm White? First I'm adopted, now I'm White?"

"Well, half White. Your dad was Black, at least that's what she put on the birth certificate. She never gave his name, just his race."

"Ha! Half. Black. Back. Blackjack," the morphine had completely taken over and as I drifted further off into la-la-land, I heard Dianne complete her story.

"We came into that NICU nursery filled with hope and saw this brave little girl hooked up to all these machines fighting for her life. Fighting to wean off all those drugs in her system. We fell in love immediately. All I could think about, all I could feel was overwhelming love. That's how you got your name - Lovey. I may not have birthed you, but you were always mine…"

**

I woke with a massive headache the next day. My parents were still by my side. They rushed to my side as soon as they saw my eyes open.

"Hey kiddo," Charles said. "How are you feeling?"

"Mmm," I grimaced in pain and lifted my arm to my head.

A plastic tube was attached to my arm and it pulled as I reached. Looking at the tube, I realized it wasn't a nightmare I dreamed up. I really was in the hospital. I really was…*adopted*. I tried shifting to get up but noticed I was still unable to move my legs. At least the pain was gone.

"Did they figure out what was wrong? Can I get my treatment and go home?"

"Not yet," mom spoke. "They are still running tests. They want to do an MRI and a lumbar puncture today."

"What's that?"

"Well, an MRI is when they take pictures of your brain. Like an x-ray, but in a machine. And a lumbar puncture, well the way they explained it is that they will put a needle in your back to get some fluid from your spine."

"That does not sound fun."

"Yes, we know honey. But it needs to be done so they can help get you better."

I nodded. I used my arms to sit myself up and with my parents help, I successfully got into a comfortable position.

"So, adopted. Why didn't you guys tell me."

"We wanted to. We even tried to, once." Dianne's smile seemed forced. "You were three and I tried to explain that I was your mom but not your real mom. You got all confused and I got all worried and I changed the subject thinking I would address it again when you were old enough to understand. After that, I never quite knew how to approach it. But you must know that we love you and always have. You are our daughter."

"Yes mom, I know. I just wish…oh, well it doesn't matter now anyway. Let's get these tests done so I can go home." I wondered about my birth parents. Were they still alive? Did I have other siblings? Did they know about me? Wonder about me? Can I meet them? But I could tell Dianne was not in the mood to discuss such sensitive matters. She put on a strong front but underneath the stress she felt from my illness was causing her to crumble.

Dianne hit the nurse call button. "Hi, umm, this is Dianne Patello from room 708. My daughter is awake and ready to get these tests done."

"Okay ma'am. I will let the doctor know," a voice called from the speaker.

Four hours later, two doctors arrived ready to do my lumbar puncture. They stood in my room smiling, setting up the equipment and explaining the procedure. Anxiety prevailed as I saw them take out tubes, needles, and medications. Dianne sensed my growing apprehension. She patted my hand and eased some of the tension. My parents helped as they positioned me on my left side, then bent my legs and lifted them up towards my chest. I jumped when I felt a cold touch on my back.

"Try to stay still," the doctor spoke with a seriousness that made me imagine if I didn't stay still, he would sever a nerve and I'd be paralyzed for life.

"Mom," I reached for her.

"It's okay baby." She got closer to me, grabbing my hand with one of hers and wrapping the other one around my shoulders. "If it hurts just squeeze my hand as tight as you can."

"Owwww," I cried as I felt a sharp pain in the middle of my back. I squeezed my mother's hand as hard as I could, but it gave me no relief. I could feel the needle being twisted around in my back, then an electrical shock shot down my left leg. "Ow!" I tried not to move. *How can I escape this pain? God. Jerome always said that prayer helps in any situation. Could it help with this? Worth a try. Heavenly Father, please take the pain away.* As I prayed the pain started to become more tolerable. *It's working. I'm going to keep going. Lord, I am so sorry for all that I have done. Please forgive me. Please help me to get better and please don't let me feel any more…*

"All done!" one of the doctors said.

I slowly opened my eyes. "That's it?"

"That's it. You did good. You're a brave girl."

But it wasn't me that got through that. Was it God? I remembered going to church with Jerome. The sermons were very intriguing. But to me, they were nice stories in a fiction book. Stories that teach lessons and get you through life. I wasn't convinced the stories were true.

Compared to the lumbar puncture, the MRI was a piece of cake. Yes, it was tight and suffocating. Yes, it was loud and made a bunch of weird noises like an experiment on an old sci fi movie, but I prayed the whole three hours I was stuck in that machine and time flew. *Hmm, maybe Jerome was telling the truth about this whole God and prayer thing. Maybe God was real. Maybe God was punishing me for sleeping with Jerome and then killing the baby that was created.* That entire night, I prayed to God for forgiveness and restoration of my health. My parents never left my side.

I woke to the sounds of a chirping bird outside my window. I could tell it would be a cloudless day. I stretched and looked over at my parents who were uncomfortably sleeping in the two chairs in my room.

"Mom, dad?"

"Yes honey," Dianne spoke with her eyes still closed.

"You guys should go home and get some rest. I'm sure it will be a while before the doctor comes to talk with us."

Charles patted Dianne's hand. "You go Hun. I'll let you know if anything happens."

"But…"

"It'll be okay. Once you get freshened up, we can switch."

Dianne kissed me on the forehead and left.

"So, Jerome?" Charles asked when my mom was out of earshot.

"Yeah."

"That was the boy who came by the house that time, huh?" I nodded. "He seemed like he was really into you. What happened?"

"He wanted to…I wasn't ready to have a baby. He moved back to Chicago after I got the…" I put my palm to my forehead in exhaustion. But when I touched, I noticed burning in my fingertips. Plus, my arm felt heavier than usual. I gasped. *Is my condition worsening?*

"It's okay. We don't have to talk about it…but just know Jerome is the one missing out. You are wonderful and if he moved back to Chicago because you weren't ready, that's his loss. Not yours."

I smiled, understanding that my dad still saw me as precious even though I had made a complete mess of my life. Who knew that one mistake could cost me everything? My life, my best friend, my boyfriend, my health.

"Lovey, your face!"

"What? What's wrong?"

"It looks droopy."

"Droopy?"

"Maybe I should call the nurse."

He did and a few minutes later Nurse Lightner and Dr. Watson came in.

"How's my favorite patient doing?" Dr. Watson asked.

"Her face, it looks…droopy."

"Smile for me," Dr. Watson commanded.

I smiled.

"Mmm, it looks like her condition is getting worse. Nurse Lightner, go grab the IVIG. We are going to start her treatment pronto."

The nurse nodded and left.

"What condition does she have exactly?" Charles asked. "Wait! Maybe I should get my wife on the phone so she can hear too."

Dr. Watson nodded and waited as dad called mom and put her on speaker phone.

"It's called Guillain Barre."

"Gui who?"

"Guillain Barre. It is an autoimmune condition. Basically, her immune system is attacking her nerves and causing paralysis. This can sometimes occur after an illness, a vaccination, or…a procedure."

Dr. Watson looked at me and I held my head low in shame. *Was my abortion the cause of this?* Dad gripped my hand giving me strength.

"So, is there a treatment? A cure?" Charles asked.

"Yes. It's called IVIG. We take antibodies from donors and inject it into her. Those antibodies fight off the diseased immune cells in her body so that she can hopefully get better."

"Hopefully?"

"Well, it's not 100 percent. Some people progress even with the right treatment."

"Progress? Progress to what? She already can't move her legs. What are we talking about? Her arms? paralysis? De…" Charles covered his mouth. He couldn't bring himself to ask if this condition could kill me. He couldn't handle that possibility.

"In some people the condition can progress to affect the arms, the face, the…lungs."

"The lungs? Like she won't be able to breathe?"

Tears started to pour from my eyes. *I did this to myself. That stupid abortion.*

"We are going to do everything we can to make sure that does not happen."

Nurse Lightner brought in a bag filled with liquid and hooked it up to my IV. She pressed some buttons on the machine I was connected to and said, "This should run over the next four hours. Let me know if you need anything."

She gave my hand a heartfelt squeeze and winked. That's when I noticed a silver cross hanging from her neck. I made it my mission to ask her about God when neither of my parents were around. That became a challenging task. My parents hovered over me like vultures on a carcass. Every move I made, they jumped to my rescue. "Are you hurting? What do you need? Should I call the doctor? Is your breathing okay?"

After a few hours of microscopic observation I finally said, "Mom, dad, I need to be alone."

"Alone?" They acted like the word was foreign to them.

"Yes, please. This has been a lot and I'm stressed. I know you guys are stressed. Maybe if you leave for a couple of hours so I can get some rest I'll feel better."

They resisted, but after several kisses, hugs, and a prolonged good-bye they left.

I reached for the call button and rang. Nurse Lightner came to my door.

"You need something honey?"

"Umm…" *How do I start this conversation? I just rang the call bell which is supposed to be used for medical needs, not to ask about her religion. Maybe I should have thought this through a little further.* "…umm. I just wanted to know if I'll be able to eat dinner tonight."

"Well, as far as I know, Dr. Watson has no more studies for you to do today so you should be able to eat something. I'll get you a menu."

She hurried off and returned within minutes handing me the hospital menu. Then she turned to walk away.

"Wait!" I spoke with unnatural enthusiasm. "Umm…you…you're…" *How do I say 'church person' without being offensive?* "…different... What's your story?"

Nurse Lightner pondered answering my question, "Well, I'm half Vietnamese and half Black. That's probably why I look different."

I snickered. "No, I didn't mean your look. I meant your spirit. Your spirit is different than what I'm used to. I…my parents are atheists. And you…you're Christian. Right?"

She smiled and grabbed her necklace. "Yes, I'm Christian."

"So, what does that mean?"

"You don't know any Christians?"

"I do…did…They aren't in my life anymore." I gulped, trying to hold back my tears. "I just…never mind."

Nurse Lightner sat at the foot of my bed. "You're curious about Christianity?" I nodded my head. "Well, what do you want to know?"

"Why did you decide to be Christian?"

She smiled as she reminisced about her journey. "I was born in Vietnam. My mom was from Saigon. My dad was an American Soldier. They fell in love during the Vietnam War. He is the one who taught my mom about Christianity and she taught me. I held onto those teachings throughout my entire life, and they really got me out of some rough situations. So, in 1989, I gave myself to Christ and never looked back."

I nodded like I understood, but I didn't understand anything. Just as I opened my mouth to ask more her pager went off.

"Up, gotta go. Room five needs their medicine."

I was disappointed. I had so many questions that were still unanswered.

"Hey! If you want, I can have the chaplain come talk to you."

I nodded.

"But it would have to be at a time when my parents aren't around. They think church folks are…" I didn't want to say naïve, stupid, gullible.

She nodded in understanding then left.

I laid there looking up at the ceiling. *Who is God? Who is Jesus? Could it be that they do exist?* I hoped the chaplain would come before my parents did. That didn't happen. But I was happy to see my parents when they walked in. Especially since they were bearing gifts – ribs from Johnny Boys, my favorite. I dug into that meal like it was my last, ignoring the fact that it took more energy to lift my arms.

The next morning I masked my pain with smiles and convinced my parents that I was well enough for them to go to work. I impatiently waited for a visit from the chaplain before their return and just as I finished my lunch tray, a thin man graced me with his presence. He was middle-aged and balding and carrying a messenger's bag.

"Are you Lovey?" I nodded. "I'm Pastor Haven, one of the hospital chaplains. Mrs. Lightner said you wanted to see me?"

"Yes. I want to know everything there is to know about Jesus."

He laughed, "Well, I'm not sure if I have enough time to tell you everything. But how about we start with one of my favorite Bible verses."

He pulled a chair close to me, then opened his bag. He pulled out his reading glasses and an old worn Bible with several sticky notes of various colors marking the pages. He flipped through the book and adjusted his glasses over his eyes.

"Ah, here it is. Isaiah 40:29-31. 'He gives strength to the weary and increases the power of the weak. Even youths grow tired and weary, and young men stumble and fall; but those who hope in the Lord will renew their strength. They will soar on wings like eagles, they will run and not grow weary, they will walk and not be faint.'"

My heart did summersaults as Pastor Haven spoke. Words had never had such an impact on me. I could feel my eyes flood with hopeful tears. *Hope in the Lord…Renew my strength…Walk. Could it really be that easy?*

"So, If I hope that God can cure me, I'll be cured?"

"Well, It's not that simple."
I knew it was too good to be true.

He went on, "God can do anything He wills – including healing you. But this verse is talking more about a spiritual healing."

"Spiritual healing? What does that mean?"

"Well, it means that you are in a good relationship with God. You can feel healed, renewed, and strong. Not physically feel, but on the inside. In here." He pointed to his chest.

"Like mental health?"

"Well, no. I mean like spiritual health. In the spirit. You have your body – that's physical health. You have your mind – that's mental health. Then you have your spirit – that's what is inside you, whether it be good or evil."

I nodded but wondered if my spirit was sick.

As if he read my mind he asked, "Do you believe in God?"

"Um, I'm not sure. All I know is when I prayed, I felt better."

"Ah, that's a spiritual healing. So, you've met God, you've experienced one of His miracles, but you are still not sure if He exists."

"Met God? I don't know about that. Me feeling better wasn't a miracle. If it was a miracle, wouldn't I be healed? And even if I were healed, who's to say it wasn't the medicine that healed me."

"Most miracles go unnoticed. I could have died in a car accident last night, but I didn't because I had to work late. That's a miracle. I took a wrong turn and discovered a cute restaurant that became one of my favorites, then five years later I meet my wife in that restaurant. That's a miracle. My parents are going through a divorce, but God blessed me with a best friend who gives me her shoulder to cry on. That's a miracle too. They go unnoticed, but they are events orchestrated by God to be a blessing to us. Subtle and overlooked, but miracles nonetheless. Even that medicine," he gestures at the hanging IV bag, "God created the person who invented it and it's being injected in your body to heal you. That's a miracle."

I had never thought about it like that before.

"Would you like to accept Jesus as your Lord and Savior?" he asked.

"I'm not sure what that means. But I'll think about it."

"Well, pray about it. Here. How 'bout I leave this with you?" He retrieved a fresh new Bible from his bag and handed it to me.

I smiled. "Thank you." Then I put it on the table next to my bed. He put his hand on my head, said a prayer, then left. I turned on my TV and flipped through the channels. Miraculously, there was nothing on that interested me. I picked up the Bible and flipped through. As I read it felt like fresh air filled my lungs and butterflies filled my heart.

Psalm 23: 4, "Even though I walk through the darkest valley, I will fear no evil, for you are with me your rod and your staff, they comfort me."

Romans 8:38-39, "For I am convinced that neither death nor life, neither angels nor demons, neither the present nor the future, nor any powers, neither height nor depth, nor anything else in all creation, will be able to separate us from the love of God that is in Christ Jesus our Lord."

John 11:25-26, "Jesus said to her, 'I am the resurrection and the life. The one who believes in me will live, even though they die; and whoever lives by believing in me will never die…'"

"Hey Squirt!" Trey said, interrupting my concentration.

I looked up to see him standing in the doorway, arms crossed and a smirk on his face. I looked at the time – 4:05. I was so engaged in my reading I must have lost track of time. I slid the book into the drawer of the table and looked up with no hint of excitement in my face or my heart.

"What are you doing here?"

His countenance changed to match mine. "Your mom told me you were here. I wanted to come and see you."

"Why?" *I mean really, shouldn't he be out trying to charm the pants off some other easily manipulated girl?*

"We were doing so good. I really thought we were, you know, getting somewhere. Then all of a sudden you just changed. You stopped talking to me. Then you go get pregnant by some other guy and I really don't get it."

I rolled my eyes. *Did he really think I was that dumb?*

"Okay, well if you want me to go I can…" he rocked back and forth trying to stall in hopes I would ask him to stay.

I stared at him blankly.

"Okay, I'll go…I'm going…I'm heading out the door…"

"Trey, wait. You can stay," I said through clenched teeth.

He smiled, nearly skipped towards me, and plopped onto the bed.

"I miss you," he said, appearing serious and sincere.

I didn't want to admit it, but I missed him too.

"Well, homecoming is coming up. Maybe you should get better so I can take you."

"Is that your way of asking me to be your homecoming date?"

"Yes."

"Real smooth genius. I'm still mad at you though."

"Uh, huh…so is that a yes?"

"No!"

"Look, whatever it is I did, I'm sorry. I just, want us to be cool again."

"We are cool. But I don't think it could ever be like what it was."

He lowered his head and I immediately felt guilt. Though why, I had no idea. He was the one who fucked up – not me.

"Okay fine, if I'm well by the time homecoming comes around, I'll be your date. As friends. But if not, can you take a whole bunch of pictures and bring them to me?"

He nodded.

Chapter 15 – Lovey October 1999

Two weeks of treatment and my condition
worsened. The doctors were stumped. My
parents were still hopeful. Me – I was tired and
weak, but I enjoyed the daily visits from Nurse
Lightner and Pastor Haven. They'd sit with me,
sing to me, read scripture, and teach me about
Jesus. Every song and Bible verse lifted my
spirits. I realized that what my parents thought
and what Erica thought about church folks were
wrong. They were not bamboozled or
manipulative. They were smart, enlightened,
loving, and beautiful people.

Pastor was sitting on the edge of
my bed reading Malachi3:3. "He will sit as a
refiner and purifier of silver…"

"Do you know what that means?" he
asked.

I shook my head no.

"Silversmiths, the way they purify silver is by holding it in the fire. The fire gets rid of all the dirt and grime contaminating the silver. They know that the silver is ready when they can see their reflection in it. Just like God. Sometimes to purify us and make us better Christians, He puts us through fiery trials. It doesn't feel good when we go through the struggle, but it is good for us. The process removes impurities from our life and from our hearts. He knows we are done when He sees His reflection in us."

As the pastor spoke, I felt fire in my bones. Not a painful burning like what I experienced when I first came to the hospital. A soothing fire. I wondered if my disease was worsening. I had little ability to move but, feeling the urge, I shifted as much as I could in my bed.

"You okay? Need me to call a nurse?"

"I don't know. I feel all hot inside. Like burning in my bones. But it's not painful."

"Oh, I know what that is. That's the Holy Spirit lighting up inside you."

"The Holy Spirit?"

I had heard of church folks catching the Holy Ghost. I thought it was all just a dramatic act. But what I was feeling was real. It was peace, love, and comfort all wrapped up in one.

"Yes, when Jesus died and went to Heaven He didn't leave us alone. He put a part of Him in each of us – The Holy Spirit. Some people suppress it. Some ignore it. But for those of us who feed it, embrace it, and listen to it, it becomes bigger, stronger, and more active in our lives."

"Well, why is it happening to me? I didn't *feed* it."

"You fed it. Every time you picked up the Bible and read. Every time you listened to a sermon and embraced the words. That was food for your soul."

"Yeah, but I'm…"

"A child of God," he stated with certainty.

I didn't feel like a child of God. I felt like crap. My heart was still heavy – filled with shame from killing my baby and filled with pain from losing my lover.

"No, really. I'm not," I responded.

Pastor Haven smiled, "Why don't you think you are?"

I had been holding my heartache in for months and, like vomit, it all came out. I confessed everything - sneaking out, hurting Erica, sleeping with Jerome, the abortion, and the pain I felt from Jerome leaving. I was a complete wreck.

Pastor Haven attentively listened to my entire story. There was no judgement on his face. There was a moment of silence when I was done. Then he shocked me with his response.

"I am a recovering cocaine addict."

"What?"

"Yeah, I started using when I was sixteen. My cousin introduced me to the drug that was supposed to take all my misery away. And it did, for a minute. But when I came down from the high I'd be consumed with finding my next fix. Then my next. Then my next. I lied, cheated, and stole just to get high again. And after the effect of each use wore off, I was back in the same empty space.

"You know, sex is a lot like drugs. It's addictive. God made it that way so husbands and wives would be bonded to each other. That bond is meant to last forever. So, when you lose a partner you have been sexually bonded with, the longing is extra painful. For a married couple, it is a beautiful thing – beneficial even. But when we take things made by God out of context, or out of season, it can be destructive.

"When you lose your virginity prematurely, you become bonded and addicted to someone who will likely not stick around. Many people fall into this cycle of trying to have more sex with more people to get over the hurt from the loss. It may feel good in the moment, but it slowly drains and defeats you. Like how cocaine did me."

"So, how did you break the cycle?" I asked.

"I found God. It didn't happen overnight. It took a lot of prayer, a lot of work, and a lot of sacrifice. But eventually I was free. And you can be too."

Tears started to pour down my face. I felt an overwhelming sense of love and peace rushing through my body. I had never felt God before; but the way I felt that day, I knew that God was real. I knew that He loved me despite my flaws and mistakes.

"Lift your hands," Pastor said.

I tried, but my arms were so weak I could barely get them off the bed. Noticing my struggle, he reached down and lifted my arms for me.

"Now repeat after me. Heavenly Father, I thank you for awakening The Holy Spirit within me. I thank you for your grace and mercy. I know that I am a sinner in need of a Savior, and I believe that you sent your son Jesus Christ as an atonement for my sins. I believe that Jesus was born to a virgin, was crucified on the cross, was buried for three days, and resurrected from the dead to save me. I accept Jesus as my Lord and Savior. Amen."

I repeated every word, and never felt more alive than I did in that moment. Pastor smiled so brightly he looked like he'd won the lottery. Then he used his handkerchief to wipe my tears away and a few of his own that had fallen.

Over the next few days I was on fire for Jesus. I wanted to read every word, listen to every sermon, hear every song, and tell the world about how beautiful it was to be in the presence of the Lord. I told the janitors, the doctors and the nurses.

"Oh, you know God? He's so good."

Some smiled and nodded. Others rolled their eyes and left. And very rarely, one would sit down and talk to me more about God's love and how He positively affected their life. I worried that my parents would condemn my newfound spirituality. But the joy I had was so overwhelming I had to let them know the truth. They were both sitting in my room watching the news like they did most evenings when the Spirit stirred within me. I felt compelled to say something.

"Mom, Dad. I have something to tell you."

"What is it honey?" my mom said.

"I…I'm…a Christian."

They both laughed. "Oh, don't be silly Lovey. You know God doesn't exist."

"Mom, I've been reading the Bible and listening to sermons. And the words…they are truth. I know it."

"Lovey," dad spoke. "Those preachers talk loud and play music that makes you feel good, but it's all psychological. It's like a magician making you think something is there but it's not. It's just a tool to get you to spend money and serve. It's an illusion."

"No. It's not a trick it's…"

"If God is real, then pray. Pray to get better." My mom stood up. Anger riddled her face.

"I have been praying for healing but…"

"And yet you are not better. See! That proves it. If God existed, He wouldn't have let this happen to you."

"And if this didn't happen to me, you'd believe in Him?"

She didn't answer. For the seventeen years that I was well, she hadn't believed in God, so why would a miraculous healing cause a change in her heart? But a sickness is what led to a change in my heart.

"God allowed me to be sick for a good reason…"

"A good reason? Charles, she's gone mad!"

"Now Dianne, we don't know that. I think she's just trying to come to terms with all she has going on…"

"No! She's gone mad. What kind of nonsense is that? 'Sick for a good reason.' That's foolishness. The doctor said that Guillain Barre could affect her mentally. Maybe the disease has gotten to her brain." My mom marched over to the call button and summoned a nurse.

"Yes?" an unsuspecting nurse asked when she entered the room.

"My daughter, the illness has gotten to her brain. We need a doctor here immediately to assess her and treat her."

"Dianne, don't you think you're overreacting a little?"

"No Charles!" Dianne's eyes filled with tears. "You don't get to tell me that I'm overreacting when my daughter is lying in a hospital bed deteriorating. It's not fair. All I ever wanted was a baby – this baby. First this so-called God made me infertile. Then we finally, finally after such a long wait get to adopt this beautiful, smart, lovely child and now He wants to take her away from me. No! No! Fuck Him! Fuck your God!"

She was sobbing uncontrollably and I laid in awe of her pain. I wished she knew that all she had to do was reach out to God and she would feel comfort. My dad got up and wrapped his arms around her. He stroked her hair.

"Shh…." he whispered. "It's going to be alright, honey."

She molded into his embrace for a few minutes then she straightened and said to the nurse, "If you could please request for the doctor to evaluate her."

The nurse nodded. "Yes ma'am."

The next day was filled with intensive testing – blood work, neuro exams, psychological evaluations and CT scans. At the end of the day the doctor came to report.

"Mrs. Patello, Lovey's condition is stable. There is no evidence that the disease is affecting her brain. And as for her psyche – it's stronger than ever."

I gloated at the report.

Mom held her head high and said, "Thank you doctor." Then she looked at me and shook her head in disbelief at the fact that I had actually become a Christian.

A couple days later Trey visited me. He was clean shaven and wearing a dark blue suite with a light blue boutonniere pinned on his left lapel. He stood in the doorway holding a matching light blue corsage and a small radio.

"Hey Squirt." He smiled and held his head high. He knew he looked good.

"Trey! You clean up nicely."

"Mmm hmm, I know," he bragged while assuming various GQ poses. I laughed at his silliness. "You stood me up."

"For what?"

"Homecoming. You said you'd be my date."

"I said if I were better, I'd be your date. I'm not better."

"You look great to me."

I rolled my eyes.

"Well, since you stood me up, I decided to bring homecoming to you."

He placed the corsage on my hand and turned on the radio. "Where My Girls At" by 702 filled the room and Trey, still holding my hand, stood up and started to dance. He swayed, spun, dipped and sang to the music.

"Go Trey! Go Trey," I egged him on.

He laughed, then sat down on my bed. "Best homecoming ever."

He pulled out some pictures from his suit pocket and handed them to me. I tried to pick my arm up but didn't have enough strength to bring it to my face. He noticed my struggle and inched next to me, holding the pictures up so I could see them.

"These are the pictures from the real homecoming."

The first picture was of him and Erica standing on her porch. She looked spectacular decked out in a long blue iridescent one sleeve dress. Her makeup and hair were flawless. She had a huge smile on her face and Trey, looking just as perfect, stood next to her with a half-smile.

"You went with Erica?"

"Mmm hmm."

My heart started to swell. He flipped through more pictures. Erica laughing. Erica dancing. Them sitting and eating and smiling and…having a great time.

"She won Homecoming Queen, too." He flipped to a picture of Erica being crowned. The photo captured a genuine look of excitement on her face.

"So, are you guys a couple now?"

"No. Why would you think that?"

I looked up to the ceiling in an attempt to hold back the tears I felt forming. I contemplated telling Trey that for the last several months I was mad at him because I saw them together.

"If your brother sins against you, go and tell him his fault, between you and him alone. If he listens to you, you have gained your brother." Matthew 18:15 ESV. The scripture spoke loudly from my heart. We were there. We were alone. And I knew that confronting Trey was a prominent step in forgiveness.

But what if he doesn't listen? I asked God.

Treat him like a tax collector.

But God, Matthew was a tax collector and he was one of your apostles.

Exactly, a repenting tax collector. He made a lot of mistakes but I didn't discard him because of his sins. I continued to love him. He learned through my love and it led him to repent. Tell Trey you love him then show him. If he repents, you have gained back your friend. If he doesn't continue to love him but from afar. Don't let his transgression bring you down. But don't hold a grudge against him either. Forgive him regardless. Love him regardless. And let him learn who I am through you.

I took a deep cleansing breath. "Trey, I saw you and Erica together…like sexually together."

His brown face flushed but he tried to brush it off and play it cool. "What? When?"

"Remember that school dance? When we saw Backyard? That night I went to your house. I planned on losing my virginity to you. Then I saw you and her, through the window. It crushed my heart."

A look of realization shone across his face. "So that's why you brushed me off?"

I nodded. First, he looked empathetic, then nonchalant, then angry. "You said you didn't want me!"

"I…I…"

"Years I waited for you and…nothing. Erica, she never rejected me. And when I was feeling down about you…" He looked at me and saw the pain he was causing me with his words and then calmed down a bit. "Erica doesn't want to be in a relationship with me. She only sees me as a friend. But that's not what I want. I want…"

"You don't know what you want."

"I do." He grabbed my hand, but I wasn't falling for it.

"Did you sleep with her? That night?"

He held his head low.

"What about homecoming?" He kept his head low.

"Mmm hmm, just as I thought. How could you want me when you've been sleeping with my best friend this whole time?"

Trey stood shook his head and said, "You know? You are so double standard. How can you forgive her but not me?"

"Actually, Erica and I aren't friends anymore either."

"Is that her fault or yours?"

My heart stopped. He was right. We weren't friends, but it wasn't because of her, it was because of me.

"Erica and I, we have our thing…" he said.

"I know." I felt lower than dirt.

"We had it before you and I started talking."

"I know."

"And when I was with you, I wasn't with her. But when you said you didn't want me, I was fair game."

"I know!"

"Look, for what it's worth, I apologize. But you can't lay here playing victim all the time when you're the one at fault." He picked up his radio and the pictures and headed toward the door. "You've gotta take responsibility for your own actions, too."

He walked out the door not looking back, and I whispered, "I know."

Nurse Lightner entered the room. "Hi Lovey!" she said cheerfully. "I was waiting for your visitor to leave before I came to turn you."

"Okay," I said, though my heart was tormented with shame.

"What's wrong with you?"

I sighed. "Trey showed me pictures of him and Erica at homecoming. She looked so beautiful and so happy and…"

"And you wish it were you?"

"No…well yes…but no. We had a falling out. I…"

"I'm sure she looked happy in the pictures, but a lot of time, people aren't as happy as they seem."

"It's not that either. I want her to be happy. I want her to have the best life. But I want to be there. I should have been there – doing her hair, taking pictures, cheering her on when she won Homecoming Queen. But I wasn't there. I couldn't be there because she's no longer my friend. And…she's not my friend…because of me," I wailed.

"It was all you? She had nothing to do with it?"

"Well, yes she did. But I forgave her. And my crime was far worse. She had Trey first. I should have never gotten involved. She had Jerome first, I should have never gotten involved. I am not in her life anymore. And the only person to blame is me."

Mrs. Lightner sat on my bed and wrapped her arms around me as I wept uncontrollably on her shoulder.

"Lovey, you've got a good heart," she said. "I know you miss your friend. But we all make mistakes. God forgives us and because of that we should all forgive each other. It sounds like you have forgiven her. Now you need to forgive yourself."

"Forgive myself? But what I did was unforgivable. I am…"

"Loved," she interrupted. "Come pray with me." Mrs. Lightner grabbed my hands and bowed her head. "Father God, we pray for strength and encouragement in Lovey's life. We pray for grace, mercy, and forgiveness. We pray that you take her broken heart and mend the pieces. We pray for healing of her heart, her mind, her body, and her soul. In Jesus' mighty name, Amen."

"Amen."

My first treatment with IVIG was a complete failure. The doctor tried to convince my mother that round two would be equally ineffective, but she refused to give up and demanded that it at least be tried. She paid for it herself since the insurance company refused to cover the cost. The treatment made me extremely nauseated. Nurse Lightner rolled me onto my side just in case I threw up. I watched as she prepared a medication to help me with the nausea. She smiled at me and winked.

"Mrs. Lightner, why did God do this to me?" I asked.

"Did God do this to you? Did the devil? Or was it the consequence of your choices?"

"I'm not sure." *Was my disease a punishment? Or a result?* "I had sex with one guy. I have friends who have slept with hundreds of guys and this didn't happen to them. I was going to be an architect. It was my dream, my destiny. But now…why did God allow this to happen to me?"

She injected the medication, sighed, then sat on my bed. "Do you know the story of Esau and Jacob?"

"No."

"Well, they were brothers - twins actually. Esau was the oldest and thus was supposed to get twice as much inheritance as his younger siblings. Esau worked hard. One time, he worked a little too hard. He stayed out hunting for the family for days and caught nothing. He came home exhausted, drained, and starving because that entire time, he had nothing to eat or drink. Jacob, noticing Esau's weakness, cooked up some stew but refused to give Esau any unless Esau agreed to give his inheritance. Esau agreed and traded a bowl of soup for his entire inheritance which, in today's economy, would be like a few hundred thousand bucks."

"Dang. That's not a very fair trade."

"Not at all. Esau traded his valuable birthright for one moment of pleasure. It probably took him five or ten minutes to eat the food. And it was stew. Meatless at that. I mean, really, how appetizing is meatless stew? It probably only satisfied him for an hour or two before he was hungry again."

"And broke."

Mrs. Lightner laughed. "Exactly. But don't judge Esau too harshly. We all make foolish trades like that sometimes. Trading our whole destiny for one moment of pleasure."

I held my head in shame, realizing I made the same mistake Esau did. I lost my health, my future, and my friendship for one moment of pleasure with a guy who up and left for Chicago without any care. Mrs. Lightner noticed my grief. She put a finger under my chin and lifted my head so my eyes met hers.

"Don't beat yourself up too much. We all make mistakes. That's not important. What is important is that we learn from those mistakes, repent, and try our best to do better."

I sniffled, knowing that for me, there may not be a next time. But if there was, I'd wait for the right guy and the right time – marriage.

Mrs. Lightner continued. "Look, I don't know why God allowed it. Maybe it was all a part of God's unfathomable plan. Maybe what you are going through will help someone else. Or maybe God just wanted you to meet me."

Mrs. Lightner giggled and tickled my tummy, which I could still feel, and she knew it. I laughed. Then her joyful countenance turned serious.

"Or maybe God wanted me to meet you…I don't know why. But I know God has His reasons."

"Hi Lovey," Erica's voice called out from the doorway.

I had a hard time turning my head to see if it was really her. Mrs. Lightner recognized my struggle and helped me turn to face the entrance. It was her.

"Erica!" I smiled.

In her right hand she held a beautiful bouquet of roses and stargazer lilies, my favorite flower. Her left hand held a balloon that read, "Get well soon!" She stood in the doorway, paralyzed with fear at my poor state of health.

"Well, don't just stand there! Get over here and give me a hug."

Erica smiled, ran over, and embraced me. I wished I could hug back but I was only able to move two fingers. A stream of tears poured from our faces.

"I'm so sorry!" we both said in unison.

"Well, it seems like you two have some catching up to do. I'll leave you alone," Mrs. Lightner said and left the room.

"I missed you so much," I whispered to her.

"I missed you too."

We hugged and cried until our tears turned into giggles. We had been far too angry for far too long. A make-up was well overdue. Erica grabbed some tissues from her purse and wiped my face, then her own.

"Girl, what took you so long to come and visit me?" I asked.

"I didn't think you wanted me to come. I thought you hated me."

"Erica, I could never hate you. You're my best friend. Always will be. No matter what. Let's promise to not ever let any guy come between us ever again."

She nodded and tried to soak up more tears with her tissue. "Lovey, I really am sorry. I should have never…with Trey…I thought you didn't want him. Shoot, I didn't want him. He was just a good fuck. It meant nothing to me. But had I known you were feeling him like that, I would have never stepped in your way. Lovey, I am so sorry."

"I'm sorry too…with Jerome…I was so stupid, thinking it was love. But…"

"Lovey don't even go there. It was love. I said it wasn't because I was hurt, angry…jealous."

"Jealous? Of me? Why? You're beautiful, smart, funny. You have men gawking at your every movement. Hanging onto your every word. You can have any man you want. No one ever wanted me like that."

"They didn't want me. They just wanted to sleep with me. That is nothing to be jealous of. It's actually something I hate about myself, meaningless sex but no true love."

"If you hate it, why do you do it?" I asked.

"I don't know. I enjoy sex. I like the attention. Or maybe it's..." she froze.

"Erica, you okay?"

"I have to tell you something. It's something I've been keeping in for years."

Her seriousness scared me. I had no idea what to expect.

"You remember Eddie? My mom's ex-boyfriend?"

"Vaguely." I tried to recall which of her mom's exes she was referring to.

She looked down and took a few deep, slow breaths in an attempt to maintain her composure. "Well, one day him and a bunch of his friends...um...they did something to me. They uh ran a train on me." Erica could no longer hold back. The tears burst from her eyes like a damn had broken. She cupped her face with the palms of her hands and held her head down in shame. I wished I could wrap my arms around her, but I laid there helpless.

"I was twelve, a virgin. That's how I lost my virginity. First Eddie started kissing me and touching me. Then he invited his friends to participate. They each took turns. I was too scared to say no. Too scared to call for help. I just let it happen. It was the worst moment of my life. I hated him for it. I hated my mom. I hated myself."

"Hated yourself? Why?"

"I trusted him. I didn't fight. I didn't say no. I let him do it and I've felt shame ever since."

"Erica, you were twelve. This was not your fault. Did you tell anyone? Does your mom know?"

"No. You're the first person I've ever told. I didn't think anyone would believe me. Eddie was a prominent member of the church we went to and he was good to me and my mom. He gave us a lot of money, clothes, shoes, and even paid our mortgage a few times."

"He was a predator," I said. "He did all that to lure you in. Why didn't you tell me? You know I would have believed you."

"We were so young. I didn't think you would understand. Plus, I was afraid you would tell someone. I didn't want to go through a court case. I see all those cases on TV with women coming forward to persecute their rapist and they pick those women apart like they have no worth. They call them liars and talk about all the bad stuff they did in the past. I didn't want that to happen to me so I pretended it didn't happen."

My heart broke for my friend. She never chose to lose her virginity. It was taken from her. "So, Eddie continued to molest you?"

"No, he broke up with my mom days after it happened. She never knew why. My mom stopped going to the church he attended which made it easier to ignore. But your past always has a way of rearing its ugly head when you least expect it. I ran into one of Eddie's co-conspirators a couple of years ago. He was an usher at one of the churches my mom and I visited. He passed me the collection plate and I froze. He didn't even recognize me. He just went on smiling like nothing ever happened. That's why I hate church. That's why I hate Christians."

"Hey, I will admit there are some not so nice people who go to church. But that is a rarity. Most Christians are wonderful people."

She looked at me skeptically. "Wonderful people who spread rumors about you, cheat you out of money, and rape little…"

She was too emotional to complete her sentence. I felt hopeless. I wished I could take her pain away. "Church will never be perfect because church people are not perfect. But God is perfect and loving and wonderful and…"

"Allows bad shit to happen to good people," Erica cut in.

"I don't know why this happened to you, but I do know that God has a plan. A beautiful destiny for your life."

Erica rolled her eyes.

"I think you should tell your mom about what Eddie did to you. Maybe she can help."

"I doubt it."

"Well, pray about it before you say no."

"I don't pray anymore. I prayed the night Eddie did that and no God came to rescue me. I don't even know if God exists."

"Erica, He does exist. I've felt Him."

"Felt Him? How can you feel Him?"

"The same way I can feel your pain. I feel Him in my heart. It's an amazing feeling. It's like warmth, love and peace all wrapped up in one. Pray with me."

Erica reluctantly took my hand and closed her eyes.

"Heavenly father," I proclaimed, "We come to you humbly asking for your grace and mercy. Father, you know our hearts and our minds. You know the number of hairs on our heads. You knew us before we were born. You know more about us then we know about ourselves. And yet with all the sinful things we have done and said, you still love us. Thank you so much for your love. Lord, I pray for my sister Erica that you will show her who you are and who she is. Lord, I pray that you heal her broken heart. That you stitch back together the brokenness she has experienced since her innocence was stolen from her. She didn't step off the porch, she was thrown off. I pray that you restore everything the devil took from her. I pray that justice is served to those who have hurt her. I pray for peace and joy in Erica's life. In Jesus name I pray, Amen."

"Amen," Erica agreed. "And Lord, if you do exist, please help my friend get better. Amen."

Erica laid her head on my chest and continued sobbing. I wanted to take away her pain but I couldn't even wrap my arms around her. All I could do was be the shoulder for her to cry on. We laid there for hours, no talking, just healing, until Erica's mom came to pick her up.

The next morning I woke up feeling overwhelming joy and peace in my heart. I felt like a heavy burden had been lifted. I smiled at two little birds that graced me with their presence as they flapped and sang on the other side of my window. Then I began to choke. I tried to yell for help but no words came out. I felt like I needed to vomit but it wouldn't come out of my mouth, it stayed in the back of my throat cutting off my oxygen. I reached for my call button with my two working fingers; but it was just out of my grasp. I wiggled my fingers in an attempt to inch closer to the device, but every time I touched it, I knocked it further away. In one last attempt I was able to wrap my fingers around the button, but before I could push it a gang of nurses and doctors ran to my rescue. I looked at them, trying to talk, but I was only able to signal with my eyes. *Help me! I can't breathe!*

Somehow they already knew and immediately went to work. They stuck a tube down my throat that sucked up all the crud lodged there. My vision started to fade but I could still hear. One of the doctor's asked if I had a pulse and then he told someone to page the respiratory tech. He said a few more words and then everything went black.

In the blackness a small light shone in the distance. The light grew until it became overwhelming and encased me. It was the brightest light I had ever seen, but it didn't hurt my eyes. I saw a figure walking towards me. As it got closer I was able to make out the most beautiful woman I had ever seen. She was holding a beautiful baby girl. She had an illuminating smile and the powerful light that shone around her resembled wings. Her presence felt oddly familiar.

"Grandma?" I said.

She looked like my grandmother, but she was young and strong, not the elderly feeble woman I remembered.

"We are here for you when you need us."

She spoke without moving her mouth, but I knew exactly what she meant. She would be there to help my transition to Heaven to ensure it was smooth. I wasn't going to die just yet, but my time was coming soon. The baby she held was the unborn child I aborted. They were both fine and happy in heaven. Erica's prayer for me was coming true. I was going to get better; but not in the way she had hoped. I was going to physically die, but spiritually live. This was God's way of me getting better and living a life where there was no more pain, suffering, or guilt. A life filled with love and peace.

"She moved. Did you see that?" I heard my mom say. "Look, her hand. It moved."

I opened my eyes and saw my dad coming towards the bed. He had tears in his eyes. It was the first time I'd ever seen him cry. I tried to speak but there was a tube in my throat. I tried to lift my arm to remove the tube but I was still only able to move those two fingers. I wanted to tell them Heaven is real, and I saw the gateway.

"Relax," mom said. "Everything will be alright."

I heeded her advice. I decided to just enjoy being with them for the few moments I had left on Earth. I spent the next several days awake, alert, and unable to speak. The tube in my throat was irritating. I prayed a lot during those days. I prayed for my family and friends. I prayed that they would find Jesus. I prayed that God would comfort them through my transition.

I had a lot of visitors. Erica and my parents spent hours with me every day. Some of my teachers and classmates came bearing balloons, get-well-soon cards and flowers. Even Trey came a few times. He didn't say much. He'd mainly sit and hold my hand. I couldn't move, but I could feel him rubbing his thumb against the back of my hand – a motion that signaled forgiveness, apology, and love.

Everyone who visited prayed for my healing. My parents initially scoffed. But as time went on, they became more tolerant of people's prayers though they still didn't believe. Despite the prayers, my condition continued to deteriorate. I developed an infection in my lungs and was being pumped with several antibiotics. My blood pressure was dropping because of the infection so other medications were being pumped through me in attempts to keep my blood pressure up to sustain life. The medications made me sleepy and nauseated. Bile was suctioned from my throat multiple times a day. I received nutrients through a feeding tube and that became painful and infected as well. My entire body was in pain.

I could feel God comforting me from the spiritual realm. He was patiently waiting for my arrival. But He did not force me to give up on living. He just sat there, radiating love, and letting me know that all would be well. I fought to stay alive. I wanted to spend as much time with my parents and Erica as the Lord would allow. I wanted to make sure they would be okay when I passed.

On the last day of my life my dad waited until there were no nurses or doctors around. Mom had gone to get something to eat so it was just he and I in the room. I could feel his warmth as he grabbed my hand.

"Heavenly Father," he said, "I don't know if you exist or not but if you do, please accept my baby into your Heaven."

I had never heard my dad pray before.

He started to cry. "Lord she is a good girl, the best girl, and I am so proud of her. Her strength and resilience have always amazed me. I am so thankful that you gave me the opportunity to be her dad. But I don't want her to suffer anymore. Please wrap her in your arms and let her know everything will be okay. Her mom and I will be okay. I really hope you exist, and I hope one day I will see my beautiful baby girl again."

He closed his eyes and wept. I could feel his thoughts. *Please Lord, send me a sign.* With the last little bit of strength God gave me, I lifted my arm and pointed to the window. My dad stood shocked and amazed at my accomplishment, then he followed the direction of my pointing and saw those two beautiful birds flapping and singing. He stared as they sang, seemingly to him. A third bird appeared as my arm collapsed and my soul left its fleshly shell to enter glory. The last thing I saw as I floated away was my dad's hopeful smile staring out the window.

Who could have known that the last two months of my life would be the most fulfilling? I spent those months in the hospital sick, paralyzed and in pain, but I was whole and happy. With the loss of my virginity, I lost almost everything. But God restores. For all that I lost, I got it all back and then some. Erica came back – her love being my treasure. I made new friends – the nurse, the chaplain, and most importantly, Jesus. I got to really know Jesus in that short time, and I fell in love with Him harder and faster than I could any lover. Then, in the end, I was reunited with my baby and my grandmother. I lost my life but gained everlasting life – a life fuller and more satisfying than you could ever imagine.

Chapter 17 – Erica December 2004

"On that morning when this life is over, I'll fly away…" the song on the radio pierced my heart. I knew that Lovey was with me. It was the same song that played at her funeral four years earlier. I wondered why her atheist parents chose such a spirit-filled song. Nevertheless, it was the perfect song. It was what Lovey would have wanted. In her last few months of life she grew spiritually. The strength, faith, and optimism she displayed while lying paralyzed in the ICU is what kept me going every day. I will never forget crying on her shoulder. It was the most comforting experience I'd ever had. It gave me the courage to talk to my mom about my rape. My mom was devastated. She felt like it was all her fault. It was a guilt that weighed heavy on her. But she used that guilt as a driver to get me the help I needed. We both went to counseling. It was a long journey, something I still struggle with. But talking to my mom and getting counseling were much-needed steps in my healing process.

The last conversation I had with Lovey was the starting point of my own spiritual journey, though mine has proven to be a lot more gradual than hers. A year after her death, I started going to church. Initially, my heart was cold and closed. I'd often sit in the back of the sanctuary listening, but only in an attempt to find faults in the sermon. Occasionally the preacher's words inspired me and seeped through the thick wall surrounding my heart. It took a while, but eventually I found a church I could identify with more than disagree with. That church emphasized Jesus' death and resurrection as atonement for the sins of those who believe. Repentance and living a God-fearing life were also stressed. I learned a lot during my Sunday attendances. But the rest of the week was still heavily influenced by the world. I was young, energized, and fun seeking. I spent Monday through Thursday taking college courses and Friday through Saturday I spent in the clubs. I had several meaningless lovers and one-night stands. For me, it was a means to get my mind off the past and revel in the present. Like a drug, it felt great at the time, but over time it left me desolate.

One of those Saturdays I went home with a handsome, smooth-talking gentleman named Terrell. I was drunk, but I knew I wanted some pleasing. I barely remember the sexual encounter we had but when I woke up the next morning he cooked me breakfast in bed. I was infatuated. We exchanged numbers and talked for a little while after that night. He let me know he was only interested in a sexual affair and I was okay with that. When I was horny, I'd call him and he'd come right over and please me. The relationship didn't go much farther than that. Then I found out I was pregnant. I was devastated. I didn't want children at all and there I was, twenty years old and not even close to finishing school, pregnant, and alone. I knew it was Terrell's as he was the only man I had slept with in months. We used protection every time, but Terrell liked it rough. He'd plow into me like my cervix was a punching bag. A few times it was so brutal the glove broke.

When I told him that he was going to be a father the response was, "So you want me to go with you to get the abortion?"

I couldn't blame him for being an asshole about the situation. I didn't want the baby either. But I thought of Lovey. I remembered how much she regretted going through her own abortion.

"I'm not getting an abortion," I boldly stated.

"Okay. Then let me know when you have the baby and I'll get a test. If it's mine, I'll help. If not, you'll never hear from me again."

Then he hung up. I tried to call back but got no answer. It didn't faze me too heavily. I had every intention on giving it up for adoption. If it weren't for my mom and Lovey's parents, I would have had to go through the entire pregnancy alone. I was blessed to have them in my corner. They were disappointed that I was having a baby so young and single. But they were supportive. They were there for each doctor appointment. They were there during the ultrasound when I found out I was having twins. They were there when I had to drop out of nursing school and go on bedrest because of complications with the pregnancy. And they were driving me to the hospital when that song came on the radio.

Not a day went by that I didn't think of Lovey. I missed her relentlessly. I felt peace when I heard "I'll fly away." I needed Lovey's presence that day more than ever. I was in extreme pain. I was worried about the health of my babies. It was too early for them to come. I was only 32 weeks pregnant, but the intensity of my contractions let me know they were coming that day. By the time we got to the hospital it was too late for any medications. The first baby was already crowning. She came out in the elevator on the way to the OB ward.

"It's a girl!" the nurse who caught her announced.

That tiny baby immediately yelled and screamed like a full-term infant. She was strong-kicking and punching as the nurse held her. The nurse used her walkie talkie to announce that assistance was needed at the elevator. When the elevator doors opened a team of nurses and doctors were waiting. They took the baby, put her under a lamp and started working on her. They wheeled me away.

Baby two didn't do so well. He was breached and his heart rate kept dropping. They planned a c-section. But before they could prep me, baby number two made his entrance into the world - butt first. He didn't cry. He was small, limp, and as yellow as a banana. I watched helplessly as a team of doctors surrounded him, placing tubes in his nose and mouth and pressing on his chest.

"Breathe, baby breathe," one of the nurses pleaded.

That little yellow hand got to me. When I saw it laying flaccid on the table I fell in love with him. It lit a fire in me. I wanted to keep my babies. I wanted to be the best mother to them. I wanted to get my life together so their life could be joyous and stable. Tears poured down my face and for the first time in years, I genuinely prayed.

"Please Lord, let him be okay."

"He's breathing," a doctor announced. "Pulse is improving. Okay. Let's go get the incubator. We'll need phototherapy as well."

A heavy pant of relief escaped my lungs when I realized his condition was improving. They were both whisked off to the NICU while the OB/Gyn repaired my third-degree tear. As soon as I was able, I asked my nurse to wheel me into the NICU to see my twins. They laid side by side in an incubator hooked up to all kinds of lines and machines.

"Would you like to hold them?" the NICU nurse asked.

"I can?"

"We encourage skin to skin contact with the mother. It helps you with your breast milk production and it helps them grow and regulate their temperature better. Wanna try?"

I wanted to, but I was hesitant. They were so small and delicate. I worried I'd drop them or break them. But the staff encouraged me, and I agreed. The nurse positioned my baby girl in my right arm first. She started sucking on my collar bone immediately. Feeling her little lips on my skin made me giggle.

"Oh my God," I said to no one in particular. "She's beautiful."

I almost cried, feeling overcome by the overwhelming love I felt attached to this little girl. The nurse then placed the boy on my left. He let out a weak little cry and I panicked.

"It's okay. He's okay," the nurse said as she positioned my arms to make him more comfortable. He stopped his cry and started to sleep in my arms.

The way you feel now is just a glimmer of how God feels about you.

I felt those words in my heart and immediately realized that God was real, and that He loves me. Tears poured. The nurses smiled.

"So, what's their names?"

I looked up at their incubator and noticed a pink tag that read girl Decker and a blue one that read boy Decker. There was only one set of names I could think of. The names Lovey told me she wanted to name her babies.

"Jordan and Jasmine," I said. "His name is Jordan Emanuel Decker and hers is Jasmine Lovey Decker."

Chapter 18 – Erica October 2007

It was warm for October and my mom volunteered to take the twins after church so I could have some me time. I hadn't had me time in months. But I knew exactly what I wanted to do. I hadn't visited Lovey since I was pregnant. And talking to her always made me feel refreshed. I walked up to Lovey's gravesite and placed a bouquet of stargazer lilies next to the tombstone.

"Hey Lovey. It's been a while. How's Heaven? Oh Earth, well you know it's Earthly. Can you believe the twins are almost three? Those little munchkins are a ball of energy. They run me ragged. But they are so sweet and so smart. Their speech is developing so quickly. Too quickly. I don't think they stop talking. I have them enrolled in swim lessons at the YMCA. Jasmine picked it up right away. She's a natural. Jordan, he still cries when I pour water on his head. They are polar opposites. But man – I love them so much.

"Me – my life is kids, work, and school. No social life for me. No love life either. But I think the sacrifice is worth it. Ever since I visited you the first time in the hospital, I had my mind set on becoming a nurse. Your nurse was so good with you. She really inspired me. Getting pregnant with the twins threw a little monkey wrench in my plans, but I'm still going to do it. Even if I can only take one college credit at a time. Terrell is not at all involved in the twin's life. He said he would help, but as soon as the paternity test came back that he was 99.99999 percent the father he stopped answering my calls. What a jerk. But we've got a court case coming up soon so hopefully that judge will make him contribute something. I've been praying because it's hard raising twins on my own.

"My mom's been supportive, but I don't want to be too much of a burden on her since she is a newlywed now. She and her husband are so cute. He does some kind of work with computers and he's really good to her. And you were right. I told mom about the rape with Eddie a couple of years ago. She took it hard. She was riddled with guilt. But we both went to counseling and started to rebuild our relationship and ourselves.

"You were right about God too. It took me a little while, but eventually I went back to church. I found one I really like. It's called 'Bethlehem Star Christian Church' pastored by Martin Lenard. The pastor is awesome. He shares the word with us and really does a great job of explaining it in a relatable way. His sermons give me hope about the future and they've led me to forgive myself and others about my past.

"Oh, and guess who introduced me to the church? Your dad! Yep. Not too long after your death he started going to church. He never told me details, but he said that he witnessed a miracle the day you died. It created curiosity in him regarding life after death. One drunken night while mourning over your death, he stumbled into the church and started cussing out Pastor Lenard who was wrapping up a Wednesday night Bible study. Pastor Lenard pulled him aside and started answering the many questions your father had about life, death, and God. After that he started visiting the church regularly. After about a year, he became a believer and was even baptized. Can you believe it? Neither can I. Your mom still refuses to step foot in a church. I pray for her often. Hopefully, she'll find her way soon.

"That about sums it up. I should be getting back to my…"

Then I realized I wasn't alone. I turned my head and noticed a man standing a few feet behind me holding roses in his hand. He straightened when I looked in his direction and cleared his throat. I didn't realize I wasn't alone, and I hoped he didn't hear too much of my life story. I squinted, he looked familiar. I stepped closer, looked closer, then realized exactly who he was.

"Jerome?"

"Hi Erica."

"Oh my God. It's good to see you. How are you? Wait. How long were you standing there?"

"Not long. Just a minute or so. How are you?"

"I'm good. I'm great! What about you? I thought you went back to Chicago."

"I did. But I usually come back here once a year – it's Lovey's death day."

I hadn't realized that, but he was right. Lovey died exactly eight years prior.

"I always come back to visit her on this day."

"You fly all the way from Chicago to visit her on this day every year?"

He giggled. "Yeah, well it just so happens that her death day is around Howard's Homecoming."

I giggled too.

He knelt down next to the tombstone and placed his roses next to my flowers.

"I miss her. I was so mad at her for…well…it was stupid. She was so young. I expected a lot from her and when she couldn't deliver, I got so angry. My hurt consumed me, and I left her at a time when she needed me the most. I'll always regret that. I didn't even know she had died until a year later. That entire year I was bitter. I spent nights cussing her out in my head for hurting me. And all that time I was hating someone who was gone. I'll never get that back."

He stood and wiped away the tears that had stained his cheeks.

"It was my fault you know – that she died. I…uh…if we had waited until she was ready. She never would have gotten that abortion and she'd still be here today."

"It's not your fault. It was just her time. She's in Heaven now so she's good." I said, rubbing his back.

He closed up, crossing his arms and stepping away from me.

"Heaven." He shook his head. "She wasn't saved. She didn't believe…"

"She did," I assured him and grabbed his hand, noticing that there was no band on his left ring finger. "In her last days she came to know Jesus well. She's the one who brought me closer to God."

He nodded, "She was my first love and my last. I haven't been with anyone since her. I truly repented and decided to wait till marriage."

I wished I could say the same but that would make me a liar and a fornicator. I had slowed since having the twins, but I was still on the prowl for some occasional fun and I hoped dearly that one of my lovers would turn out to be Mr. Right.

"Well," he broke our silence, "at least you made your amends before…" he looked at her gravesite then looked at me. "I didn't even get a chance to say goodbye. Anyway, it was nice talking to you Erica. God Bless."

"God bless." I waved him away then leaned over Lovey's tombstone and whispered, "I love you, Lovey. And I miss you so much. Rest in peace my angel."

The End

Acknowledgements

First and foremost, I would like to thank God for blessing me with the inspiration to write three novels that hopefully have been a blessing to you.

Thank you, reader, for taking a chance on an indie author and reading this book. If you enjoyed the book, please leave a nice review. It is extremely helpful and much appreciated.

Thanks to my hubby lover friend who has been there with me through thick and thin. He has been the shoulder I've cried on for many nights. He always knows the right words to say when words are needed to soothe my soul.

Thanks to my three crazy children who brighten each day.

Thanks to my inspirational mother who is a tremendous help and has always been in my corner.

Thanks to my three best friends for all the laughs we have shared and all the trials we have hurdled over together.

To all the friends and family I have lost along the way, I miss you and love you. May God bless you always.

More from Amy Watkins

200 Letters

Cute for a Black Girl